Sister Waterma[n]
Merry Christm[as]
Thanks for everything
Dallan Adams

The Light in the Room

Novels by Marilyn Brown

The Earthkeepers series:
Thorns of the Sun
Shadows of Angels
Royal House

Good-Bye, Hello
Statehood
The Wine-Dark Sea of Grass
House on the Sound
Ghosts of the Oquirrhs

Sharing Christmas collection:
Christmas at the M&M
The Holly Christmas
The Macaroni Christmas Tree

The Light in the Room

A Novel by Marilyn Brown

Springville, Utah

Copyright © 2003 Marilyn Brown
All Rights Reserved.

No part of this book may be reproduced in any form whatsoever, whether by graphic, visual, electronic, film, microfilm, tape recording, or any other means, without prior written permission of the author, except in the case of brief passages embodied in critical reviews and articles.

ISBN: 1-55517-637-2
v.2
Earlier version, 1984, *Good-bye, Hello*
Published by Salt Press
Imprint of Cedar Fort Inc.

Distributed by:

Typeset by Marny K. Parkin
Cover illustrations by Simeen Brown
Cover design by Nicole Cunningham
Cover design © 2002 by Lyle Mortimer

Printed in the United States of America
10 9 8 7 6 5 4 3 2 1

Printed on acid-free paper

Library of Congress Cataloging-in-Publication Data

Brown, Marilyn McMeen Miller, 1938-
  The light in the room : a novel / by Marilyn Brown.
     p. cm.
  ISBN 1-55517-637-2
  1. Reminiscing in old age--Fiction. 2. Terminally ill--Fiction. 3. Aged women--Fiction. I. Title.PS3552.R694 L54 2002
  813'.54--dc21
                                                    2002014753

For my nieces and nephews and their cousins.
And for all of their children and grandchildren—
who can be proud of this great grandmother.

1

*I*t would soon be Christmas, 1963. There was a taste of cinnamon and apples in the air. Elizabeth Ann Wood Preston, almost ninety years old, may have been confined to her bed, but she could still smell the clove and nutmeg in the kitchen, and the sharp heady pine scent of the little decorated Christmas tree her daughter Clara had put in the corner of the room.

Elizabeth Ann knew a Christmas when she saw one. But she had never seen one so bright. Moving in and out of a troubled sleep, sometimes all she could see was light. There was so much light, she wondered if she had already gone to heaven. But Clara's voice in the kitchen, a honk in the driveway, and a roller skate in the hall, told her no. Not yet.

Oh, she had somehow suspected that it wouldn't be long now. But for some reason, whenever she turned her head toward the Christmas tree—even with her eyes closed—she saw a stranger standing in the room.

Like her grandmother, who had cried out "Hello, Thomas Gregory!" when she died, Elizabeth Ann expected to see someone come for her. She hoped it would be Owen, who had already been gone eight years. She certainly hadn't expected a stranger.

There were many people she had been anxious to see on the other side—the people important to her besides Owen. There would be Mama and Papa, and all of her brothers and sisters: tall skinny John, sister

Jennifer with the straight nose, Laura with the braid down her back, sandy-haired Peter, and little Farrell. She would have recognized any one of them, even Clothilda. She still felt that stab of pain when she thought about Till. She never expected to see Till again. Funny how even the years did not erase that pain.

Well, she wasn't going to think about Till anymore. She'd spent too many of her Christmases wondering and worrying about Till and Rye. It had been Christmas when the sweethearts had married so long ago. And it had been Christmas when Elizabeth Ann went to California to view Till dressed in navy blue, a dark shape in the white coffin. She had always worried about Till in California. "Well, when there's one sheep missing, that's the one you go after," Papa had always said, and he was a shepherd; he ought to have known.

Instead of concentrating on Till, she ought to think about Owen. And for the last few weeks—when she had become very ill and knew she would soon be going—she anticipated seeing Owen. She imagined that he would be standing with all of the others close by, ready to greet her. She would be a newcomer on the other side. Her family would be right there to show her around. That was her plan.

And then—though she was not sure her eyes were open or closed—she saw this strange man.

Well, he was somebody from the past, but she couldn't recognize who. In white robes he was standing just off the floor holding out his hand. Why? This was something she had to think about for a while. She had certainly decided now wasn't the time to go.

At least she didn't think she had crossed over yet. Or had she, anyway? She thought she was waking up in the world as she knew it, but she realized she still hadn't opened her eyes.

Beginning as far back as she could remember, she had tried to live a good life—and for the most part she had done well. But every perfect plan she had ever made had seemed to have some flaw in it. It had been part of her plan not only to be greeted by Owen, but to leave from her own little house in the backyard—not from the big family house in front, where it was easier to bother the grandchildren at Christmastime with this and that trouble, or this and that need or pain. But her plans hadn't exactly materialized. It was only last night that the pain had flared up so severely that Clara had insisted that Grandma be moved to the big house—at least for Christmas. David had fetched the sheriff, and they'd wrapped her up in the feather ticking and made a stretcher out of Owen's army blanket pinned over the mop and the broom handles. They'd carried her from her little house out in back through the doorway across the yard to the house where Clara's family lived. On the way, while they were hauling her, she had joked with the sheriff, laughing, "This is a first. I never been put out of my house by the sheriff before!"

"Shh. You've been very sick, Mother," Clara had whispered. Clara bent down to her, touching her cheeks, her face wet with tears. Well, Elizabeth Ann thought, it wasn't easy to leave people who didn't want you to go, and especially if you saw somebody you couldn't quite remember about to take your hand.

But where was she now? Imagine not knowing! She was either in heaven or in some room of Clara's house. But she was still not quite sure. That was silly. All she had to do was open her eyes and find out. In a minute I'll open my eyes, she thought. But she waited until she was good and ready. She lifted one eyelid. She opened one eye the slightest bit, peering through her stubby eyelashes. Then, barely opening both eyes, she shut them again quickly. The blinding white light had to be from more than just the Christmas tree. And now there seemed to be a large dark spot in the middle of the white. Perhaps that strange man had left something dark in the middle of it.

Or maybe that's the page that has my report on it, she thought. My life's over, and there I go with my white page and a spot on it.

She made a great effort to focus. And she smiled. But it wasn't a spot. It was four-year-old Robin's curly head. Her youngest granddaughter was standing over her. Clara had put her into Robin's nursery. Elizabeth Ann wasn't much better equipped for life than a baby, anyway. She might as well be in a nursery. Life was a circle. Somebody finally took care of you all over again.

"Hello, Grandma," Robin said.

"Hello, darlin'."

"Did you wake up, Grandma?"

Elizabeth Ann concentrated on Robin's eyes. She wanted to start up a conversation, but all she could do was to send feelings of love. It's you and me trading places now, Robin, she thought. You go and find out what life is all about. I am going to my family. They are all somewhere in that light that's come into the room. . . . Well, almost all of them are. She squinted. She was still seeing things.

No, she wasn't on the other side yet, but maybe she was now getting ready to take that leap. She closed her eyes again. If she could just go calmly—whether she met anyone or not—something might happen. And something did. She began remembering what happened when she was Robin's age. She began to remember her family, though they had all passed on before her—even her younger brother. She was getting ready to see them now—except for Till. She closed her eyes.

But a little voice broke her concentration. "Don't go, Grandma." Robin touched her hand. "Don't go."

Elizabeth Ann looked up. There he was again. She couldn't believe it. There was that same man! Maybe she would remember who he was. She thought she heard him say something, "I wanted to tell you a few things. It took us a long time, but . . ."

But what? With her granddaughter Robin by her bed trying to hang onto her, Elizabeth Ann wasn't about to take that young stranger's hand.

She was almost irritated. "If you come to tell me a few things, one of them ought to be your name."

"I just come to ask you if you forgive us. Did you, Annie Wood?"

Annie Wood. She hadn't heard anyone address her by her childhood name in years. Who was this? And what did he have for her to forgive?

She looked up at him. Was she in the future or the past? Again she couldn't tell, though she sensed she was clinging to Robin's fingers.

All at once, in another bright light, a day from long ago spiraled up into her vision. And suddenly the past was flooding over her. She could not hold it back. In the light she thought she could see someone who looked like the stranger. Was that the face? She couldn't tell.

It was spring in Antimony. Something had happened the day she cut the blossoms out of the apple tree. She had done wrong. While all of the others had gone to Kingston to grind the wheat, Papa made her stay home alone with Till. Clothilda was eighteen then. Elizabeth Ann was four. Papa had been so angry with her. "The pruning that needs to be done is on you, Elizabeth Ann Wood," he had shouted. "To prune out some of that mischief. You can stay home with Till—upstairs in the girls' room in the loft. You ought to have a long think about what you did."

She felt like somebody had poured lead inside of her limbs. As the wagon drove away, she had been afraid to raise her guilty eyes to her big sister Till. When she finally looked up, she saw that Till was studying her through tangles of her shiny dark hair. Papa always said that Till was "too pretty for her own good. Too many boys after her already. The pretty ones get plucked before they're ripe, like a green apple."

Till had tried to be kind to her little sister Annie. She had put her hand on Annie's shoulder, though Annie felt it burn through her dress like a reproach. "You did wrong, Annie," she said. "But you'll learn what's right from wrong someday."

But someday wouldn't do any good. She was going to miss out on today.

"If you accept your punishment today, Papa might take you to the lumber mill tomorrow when he fetches the boards to build onto the kitchen," Till continued. "And then to Aunt Dora's to see your cousins. But you have to learn right from wrong. And to obey."

Papa had told Annie to go upstairs and stay there. Grieving, she sat on the top step while the others got ready to go. She was trying to be obedient, to keep her feet off the second step. But peering down the steep staircase, she could easily see the table. On it sat the milk pitcher with the sprays of apple blossoms, silver white in the sunshine, making the dusty little kitchen look like a garden. It was just as she had imagined when she cut the blossoms this morning. Till was sweeping the floor. Cloudy dust rose and fell, shimmering in the sunlight around the apple flowers like stars. Mama had lamented that Annie had cut off all of the new branches, and that now it would take more than a year to grow back what she had cut.

When Annie watched them all leaving for the mill in the cart—John, Jennifer, Laura, Peter, Farrell, Mama, Papa—her stomach cramped up into an empty pain. All of them were gone now, except for Till.

She sat for a while thinking about the pain when the strangest thing happened. She heard a horse clattering into the yard. When she bent down from the top step to get a look through the outside window, she could see a young man, his choppy hair blowing all over his head. He leaped down from the old horse as though he were a knight in silver armor. Did she recognize the young man's face? *She stared at the image in her mind. Was that the face?* Still sitting on the top step, she clamped her arms shut on her stomach, holding in her deep, sad pain.

Till burst through the door. The young man leaped toward the steps, and suddenly seized Till roughly around the waist. Annie gasped in horror, cold gripping her scalp. *Till! Till!* They were holding each other so fiercely Annie was afraid he was choking her. Annie's own breathing stopped.

"My darling," he whispered hoarsely. "I came as soon as I could. You told me . . ."

"Yes, yes," Till whispered. "Shhh. . . . They left Annie with me. Upstairs. Quiet. I love you."

I love you. It must have been all right. Annie still wasn't breathing, but her heart clattered against her ribs. *I love you.* What a strange way of showing love.

Slowly, barely moving, she backed up the steep stairs and into the girls' room. Her heart beat wildly, as though she had seen something she should never have seen. She lay down on the cot under the stuffy attic bedroom roof and stared at the pine rafters for hours. She read books, picked up her embroidery, and drifted in and out of sleep.

Finally, when it was dark, she heard Papa with the cart in the henyard and Mama coming through the door. They were home. She pretended to sleep while they came into the loft bedroom carrying something big—a package they slipped along the floor boards under the eaves of the roof. She was going to get up out of bed and tell them what had happened to Till, but they were so quiet that she stayed quiet until Papa finally called her down to their late supper.

Annie didn't breathe a word to Papa about the man who kissed Till. She was sure no one knew about it, because on the next day, when Till said brightly she would help Papa load at the lumber mill if John didn't want to go, Papa looked up from his newspaper and, without blinking an eye, said, "All right."

Annie stood by listening, trying to stand in Papa's line of vision. He noticed her. "And because Annie stayed upstairs all day like a good girl, I guess she can come, too."

Annie thought the top of her head would come off. "Oh, thank you, Papa. Thank you."

But she could also feel a little fear. She knew in her bones that Till was thinking of something else besides helping Papa at the mill. For one thing, Till was taking much longer than usual fixing her hair.

Even Mama might have suspected something was going on. "Till!" she called from the bottom of the stairs. "You're keeping your father waiting!" She sounded irritated and disapproving. "You'd think she is fixing up to see the king of England. Goodness knows she's too pretty to need improvement. Go and fetch her, Annie!"

Annie slowly climbed the stairs. She was also anxious for Till to hurry so they could get going. She pushed open the door into the hot attic room. Till sat looking into a little looking glass propped up in front of a rock. She was pinching her cheeks.

"Papa says to hurry."

"I'm coming, Annie," Till said, not turning to look.

"You look pretty," Annie said. Standing behind Till, Annie saw her own reflection in the mirror. Her hair was not bright brown like Till's. It was scanty, and the color of dry wheat. Her nose was straight, and her eyes large for her face. She watched Till pinch and fuss until there were roses in her cheeks.

"Tell Papa I'll be there in a minute," Till said.

Annie backed into the dark closet under the eaves pretending to be gone.

"You're still here, Annie," Till said crossly.

Annie bumped against a big burlap-wrapped package. She had almost forgotten that hazy moment during yesterday's nap when Mother and Daddy had brought something large and shoved it under the rafters.

"Come out of there, Annie! Those are surprises! And you won't . . ." Till stopped. "Come out of there at once! Hurry! You're not obeying!"

Surprises! *For who, what?* One of those surprises might be for her! And here she was, not being obedient again.

"Well, then, we'll just leave you," Till said, and she started down the stairs.

Annie hustled after her toward the cart just as Papa was about to pull away.

Up the Antimony Canyon a piece, the road narrowed into a smaller trail that ended in Mr. Wilcox's mill squatting over a dark pond. As Papa drew the cart up to the stacks of lumber, Till stood atop the wagon ready to guide each cleanly cut piece to the load while Papa and Mr. Wilcox hoisted.

Not long after the loading commenced, Annie saw the same young man who had kissed Till yesterday. He came out of the mill, his white teeth bright between his smiling lips.

"Papa," Till began, then swallowed. "I want you to meet Rye."

Annie stared. *Rye? Like bread?*

"I know Rye," Papa said, not showing much interest. He hoisted another piece of timber into the air. The young man lifted the end of it and Till jumped down from the cart.

"Rye," she whispered to the young man. "Tell him, Rye."

Mr. Wilcox, the owner of the mill, practically catapulted himself off the ground with a sneeze. "I swear, this lumber breathes sawdust into your inside parts until you can't get air anymore." While he was talking to Papa, he wiped his brow with his sleeve.

As Rye came up to the men, he waited awkwardly. "Mr. Wood . . ." he stammered, trying to interrupt.

But Papa Wood was in an earnest conversation with Mr. Wilcox. And now Mr. Wilcox was smiling at Till, trying to get her attention. "Your pa and I were old drinking buddies," he grinned at Till. He dusted his hands against his pants. "Them days are over, right, John Wood? Once you associate around the Mormon Church you don't make drinking buddies anymore."

But Till wasn't listening. Her eyes were wide and anxious. She was watching Rye. "Rye," she urged.

"The Mormon Church teaches a man to forsake his old ways and make new friends, live the life of a civilized human being, the spiritual man. Isn't that right, John Wood?"

"I'll be in agreement with that," Papa said.

"You don't have much use for the old friends anymore."

"Papa, Rye and I wondered . . ." Till broke in.

"Is that all, Brother Wood?" Wilcox slapped his thighs. The dust rose in clouds from his pants.

Annie wondered if she should be hearing this weighty conversation. She sat down on the road and picked at a mound of old mushrooms with a sharp pointed stick. The puffs broke apart like dry cheese.

"I believe so," John Wood announced. "That new kitchen will go up in no time. Nice to see you again, Wilcox, and you, young Hadley. I won't be seeing your pa, young man, but it don't hurt to say a Christian hello." He leaped into the wagon, leaving Till and Rye standing together alone.

Rye blushed. "No, you won't be seeing my pa, Mr. Wood. My pa's been dead these two years."

Papa's eyes suddenly lost their brightness. "Oh. That so?" he murmured. "I'm sorry, boy." He turned. "Get into the wagon, Till. Get over here, or you'll get left behind."

Annie poked again at the mushrooms.

"Annie!" Papa barked.

She turned and saw one glimpse of Rye Hadley's dark eyes. He was glaring at her. Not for any particular reason. Just glaring. Till was wringing her hands.

"I'll tell my mother hello for you," Rye stammered.

Till did not get into the wagon, but stayed by Rye, her sleeve brushing against his arm. For a brief moment there was a very loaded silence. Almost imperceptibly, Till nudged Rye Hadley at his elbow. Finally Rye continued. "And I might . . . I just might sometimes come to call on Till . . . if that'd be all right, sir." Now the silence was even heavier. It seemed as quiet as a stone while the realization of what was happening began to register in Papa's eyes.

"Uh . . . that won't be necessary," Papa finally said. "Good-bye now. Tell your ma hello."

But Till didn't want to let it go. "Papa," Till forced the words. "Rye wants to come. May he please come?"

Papa's eyes narrowed. "Come callin'?" He stood back. With his mouth in a dark line, he said the words quickly. "I don't think so."

It was the good-natured Mr. Wilcox who took the risk of stating his enlightened opinion. "Oh, now, I doubt it'd hurt once to come callin'," he laughed. "My own son come a-callin' on several girls just to pass the time of day."

Papa scowled. There was a very long pause. "Well, I suppose if he has to come, he has to come."

"Oh, Papa, thank you, Papa," Till breathed. She bounded into the wagon, her eyes fastened on Rye, her cheeks glowing.

Papa clucked to the horse. "Good-bye now. Thanks so much, Wilcox. I'll be back to pay you what I owe you."

Till looked toward the far hills. She tilted her chin.

Papa said, "Too bad that boy looks like his pa. The man wasted his life away. Any boy of his will be no good too, I tell you. Irresponsible. A lady's man. Wilcox has told me some things. You'd be better off not coming much near the likes of him."

Till was silent all the way home.

2

*S*ilent night, holy night. Elizabeth Ann could hear the strains of the choir music from the front room phonograph. The music of Christmas was her favorite. It wafted over the sound of Robin's tricycle and the washing machine, the clank of dishes in the kitchen and the whir of David's drill in the garage.

After Robin had left the room, it seemed a long time before anyone else came, and a long time that she kept her eyes closed. Now she opened them again. She was surprised. She couldn't see that strange face anymore. Maybe it was not the same man. She was not sure. She hadn't seen him for years and years, not since he went off to California and left the Church. So she couldn't tell. Yet the memory of that day had been so clear.

That night after their return from the mill, the family sat together in the big room by the fire just before dark. Peter and John had just carried the last bucket of slop out to the hogs, and little Farrell had followed them. Mama had begun to twist and sew the rags in her basket for her new rug. Nobody said anything, but everybody was wondering if Rye Hadley would really dare to come. Till was sitting in the window seat pretending to knit while she watched toward the post office in their nearby town of Coyote.

"If these nights wasn't so cold, we'd have good

weather now," Mama was saying.

"All things come in their due season," Papa answered. "It'll be warm soon enough." He stood over the warm coals in the fireplace, his elbow on the mantel. The coals lit up his face with orange light. He kicked the wood gently with his shoe. "We'll have to have more chips to start it up tomorrow."

More chips. No one liked to collect the wood chips. All of them knew Papa was getting ready to ask somebody to collect more chips.

"It's Annie's turn," Laura said, pushing her dark braid out of the way. On the floor in the corner, she was making rope out of the stringy cedar bark they had collected last fall.

"It's not either."

"It is. Ask Till or Jenny." Laura looked at Jennifer, who was sitting on the hearth tatting.

"Don't matter whose turn it is. It's got to be done," Papa growled. "Annie!"

"It isn't my turn. It's Farrell's. I did it last time."

"Farrell's too little!" Laura said.

"He's not. He did it once, Mama."

"Farrell's out with the boys taking the slop to the hogs," Papa said.

Mama turned. "Those boys have been gone plenty long enough. Go fetch them, Jennifer."

Jennifer was sixteen and tall. Not as pretty as Till or Laura. She and Annie both had Papa's straight nose. "They'll come, Mama."

"I worry about Farrell. He was sniffling yesterday. If he comes down with something, he won't be going with us to Aunt Dora's next week. The rest of her children might catch something. . . ."

Catch something. In the past couple of years, Annie had learned that several of Aunt Dora's children had died of catching something. Mama had told her that Aunt Dora and Uncle Al would go to the endowment house or the temple when it was finished someday, seal their children to them, and raise them after they were dead. Annie found it very puzzling. But her cousins Katy, Pauline, and Jeremy were left. Katy and Pauline were the ones she liked to visit.

"Are we going to Aunt Dora's?" Annie stood on the rocker of Mama's chair and rocked with her. "Can I go? Can I go?" She had a suspicion that one of the surprises in the attic was for Katy's birthday.

"Yes, we'll probably go to see Aunt Dora soon—maybe next week," Mama said. "And yes, you may go if you're good, Annie. If you're good . . . remember?"

Suddenly, at this point, Till leaned forward.

Papa's eyes darted to Till. "Is that your young snip coming up the road?" All of them were quiet. Under his breath, Papa said angrily, "I don't like that young snip setting a foot in this house. But I'm not sure what I'm going to do about it."

It was Rye, all right.

Till turned, blushing. "You said, Papa. . . ."

"I know. I said if he had to come, he had to come."

"Ma!" Till turned to Mama. "Please don't let Papa say awful things. Please make Papa let Rye in the house." Till's fingers grew tight on her knitting needles.

"Now, girl. Don't get all worked up. Your Papa will do what he will do. He keeps a pretty good hold on his temper."

"Mama!" Till was clearly worried.

"The days I make your papa do different from what he wants to do are long gone. If he scares Rye Hadley away, we'll know it's for the best."

That didn't help Till. Clutching her knitting needles, she rushed to open the door.

Rye Hadley looked washed and clean, with his hair combed, except for a stray lock that had fallen in his eyes during his rugged ride. He moved toward Till, grinning. She brought him in by his elbow.

"It's good of you to come, Rye."

"My pleasure," Rye breathed hard. "Hello, Mr. Wood, sir." Papa walked up to him slowly, and Rye's grin disappeared.

"Hello, Rye," Papa said with surprising good will. "Won't you come sit here and chat with us?"

"It's my pleasure, sir. I will, sir."

Till looked like a blossom in the ruffled blouse Mama had made for her from an old tablecloth. A sash of satin circled her waist. Following Rye Hadley, knitting still in her left hand, she sat beside him on the settee.

"Well," Papa began.

"The weather's good, ain't it?" Rye Hadley tried.

"Yes, it is."

"You ought to make good time putting up your extra room."

"Yes, I should."

"Until it gets hot."

"It's hot daytimes."

"But the nights is still cold."

"Yes, they are."

Mama looked at Papa, her brows raised. "How's your good mother, Rye?" Mama asked.

Rye blushed. "Not well since Father died. Thanks."

"Are you still working at the mill?"

"Yes, I am," he said. Mama's kindness seemed to loosen Rye a little. He looked at Papa hesitantly. "I meant to talk to you about something . . . I wanted to ask . . ."

All of them waited, breathless, but it was plain

that Papa did not want Rye to say anything while everyone was present. Annie hid back behind Mama's rocking chair, but it was no use.

"Run along, Annie," Papa said. "Laura, take Annie out and help her get the night wood, the chips. Run along, the two of you."

"It's not my turn," Laura said, looking at Annie and then at Rye. "Papa, it's not my turn. Annie can go. I'll stay here."

Papa looked stern. Then he spoke in a low steady tone that cut off argument. "I'm talking to both of you. Laura, you can round up Jennifer and the boys. Annie, you bring the chips. But both of you get out. Now."

Laura stalked out. "The pan, Annie," Papa said. He pointed to the chips pan in front of the hearth.

Annie looked over at Till perched on the settee beside Rye. Till was still red around her ears. Her hair was curled on top of her head like the girls in town did it now. She looked pretty.

"The pan, Annie," Papa pointed to it. She reached down to the pan, dumped the few slivers into the fireplace, and walked slowly, straining to hear a few words. But Rye said nothing.

"Hurry, Annie."

"It's about . . . well, it's about . . ." Rye began. Annie hesitated, but he stopped until she got past the door, and then she could barely hear his voice. "I got a question to ask you, sir."

"Well, I have some questions I want to ask you, Rye Hadley," Papa boomed. Then there was a little moment of silence before Papa yelled, "Annie! Get those chips! Hurry. When you're done, you can come back."

There was no way to fool Papa.

Laura was outside calling to Jennifer and the boys. They were watching the piglets root for their dinner. Farrell was laughing. Annie swung the empty pan by its edge hard against her skirts. She hated Laura for making Papa think it was her turn to gather wood chips. She hated to gather wood chips, and it really wasn't her turn.

Around the bottom of the cutting stump were thousands of chips scattered in all directions. Mama said sometimes you have to do things you didn't want to do, and the secret to happiness was to learn to want to do those things. But Annie didn't want to like picking up wood chips. She sat by the stump with the big pan in her lap. Trying not to get the dirt under her fingernails, she carefully scraped up the little bits of wood and threw them into the pan. They hit the metal like popcorn.

Down near the hog yard she could hear the others laughing.

"Shall we, then?" John hooted.

"Let's go. Let's go. I want to go," little Farrell chanted.

"Shhh," Laura cautioned. "They'll hear us!" she shrieked. Everybody leaned forward, heads together. Annie could not hear what they said. But when they started away from the fence, Laura yelled, "Then just stay here, Jenny!"

"You'd better stay here, too, Laura—you and the rest of you!" Jennifer grabbed at John, but he wrenched himself free. "Stay here, I tell you. It's none of your business what Rye Hadley asks Papa!"

But she was too late. John and Peter ran to follow Laura around the other side of the house. Farrell stumbled after them. Annie could see they were going to sneak under the parlor window. If Laura hadn't made her get the wood chips, she'd be there under the window, too.

From a wide circle around her, most of the wood chips were gone. She needed to move somewhere else, but she didn't want to find any more wood. She watched everybody giggling beneath the parlor window, and it made her angry she wasn't there. She took a big dry piece of bark and started shoveling up the chips along with a lot of dirt. She did it fast so that she could pretend she didn't know how much dirt was going into the pan. She didn't care. Papa wouldn't even know. A pan of dirt looked almost like a pan of wood chips.

The others were still laughing. Jennifer was telling them to be quiet. Quickly Annie arranged a covering of wood chips to hide the dirt. Holding the pan with both hands, she got to her feet and stumbled a little way down the hill, sometimes slipping and sliding in the dust, keeping her steps small to steady herself. The pan of dirt was heavy.

At the back door she waited a minute before she stepped into the house. She saw Papa stalk toward the front door and open it wide. Rye Hadley followed Papa, and she could hear Till crying.

Papa's voice was loud. "You haven't got any right, boy. No, you haven't got any right to say what Till wants or doesn't want. I'm in charge. And I say she's not ready for the likes of you with your shiftless working habits and your liquor."

Rye stepped out into the fading daylight. The sun was perched on the edge of the mountain, getting ready to spill over to the other side of the world.

"I'm sorry, Mr. Wood. Honest. I'm sorry. I'll reform. For Till I'll do anything I can. Just give me a chance!" Half stumbling, Rye backed away from Papa and toward his horse. Papa stopped at the front door and leaned out, looking ready to chase Rye down the road. But Rye climbed up quickly and rode away.

For a while Papa waited. Finally he said, quiet-like, "Says he can't help himself. If there's anything I can't tolerate, it's a man who can't help himself. What kind of a man can't help himself?" Papa turned back into the room.

Mama got up out of her chair. "John, you've made Till cry."

"She'll get over it," Papa snapped. Then he walked to his chair.

Annie was afraid to go inside. Papa was shouting at Till to forget Rye and start thinking of other things. He didn't say what. "Just you think of him like he was dead."

Mama was holding Till's head on her shoulder, patting her hair, saying, "It's all right, Till. If he loves you, he'll change and come back."

Still sobbing, Till turned to Papa. "I won't stand for it, Papa. You're treating me like a child. I have my own life to live."

Papa began to steam up. "Clothilda Wood!" His eyes narrowed. "That's enough out of you. You're still too young to make a choice for a lifetime. For eternity, as far as that goes." Eternity was a very long time. While most couples in these parts got married by the bishop first, a lot of them were going up to the Salt Lake endowment house after a few years to be married forever. Mama and Papa had taken the family up four years before Annie was born. Mama had told her about it when Annie had asked about Aunt Dora's dead children. "Sealing is forever," Mama had said. "Forever is a long time to be stuck with somebody if he isn't true blue."

Papa was still almost yelling. "You think you've got your mind made up on Rye Hadley, but Rye Hadley is no choice."

Till stopped crying, stood up, and looked Papa straight in the eye. "No, you wouldn't choose him," she said slowly. "But I would, and I do. I love him. If he isn't good enough for you, what does it matter? I'm the one who has to live with him." At the end, tears came into her voice again, and she turned to Mama. By this time Annie, dumbfounded, was standing in the doorway. The others began to come in, too. Mama saw Annie first.

"Put the chips down, Annie," she said. "My, that's a nice big pan you gathered."

Annie knew she had cheated putting the dirt in the pan, but she didn't say a word. She watched Till sobbing against Mama's shoulder. When everyone came into the room, Till ran upstairs. Papa stood in front of the window with his back to them.

"Put down your chips. That's a good job," Mama said again.

Carefully Annie placed the pan on the hearth, but it was so heavy, it made a thud.

"I think we'd better get Till away from here," Papa was saying to Mama, his back still to them. "She needs to get a bit older so she can see straight. Do you suppose you ought to go ahead and take her up to Dora's for a week sooner than we planned—get her thinking of something else?"

Mama gathered up the rags from her rocking chair and sat down. "I don't know, John Wood. Sometimes you amaze me. But you may be right."

"Can you start off tomorrow?" He turned and looked at Mama squarely.

"Yes, I suppose we can," Mama said, the rags and the needle quiet in her hands. "Whatever you think is best."

"Take Annie and Farrell and spend maybe a week.

Get Till used to the idea it's not going to hurt anything to wait—to grow a little. Maybe she'll forget."

Aunt Dora's! Annie thought about how much she had wanted to be included when they took the trip to Aunt Dora's. She swallowed hard.

"We'll start in the morning, then." Mama brought her sewing up close to her eyes to see how she was doing.

All of a sudden Annie felt awful. It was that pan of dirt, and Mama saying, "That's a good job." Annie fastened her eyes on Mama rocking gently. Papa was still standing by the window, his hands in his pockets. "Get to bed, children," he growled.

"Aw!" John complained.

"No arguments! Get to bed, I say." He turned his head toward them briefly.

"Can't we hear what you're going to do?" Laura asked.

"Going to do? There isn't a thing to do. Nothing." Papa still watched at the window.

"I mean, what is going to happen to Till and Mr. Hadley?"

"That's what I mean," Papa said. "Nothing."

With half her mind Annie thought about what they were saying, but in the other half she was wondering how she could take her dirt pie out to the woodpile again without Mama seeing her. If Papa discovered the dirt in the wood chips, she wouldn't have half a chance of going to Aunt Dora's in the morning to see Katy. Last time she was there, they found birds' eggs in a nest hanging over the edge of the river.

"Can't we stay up until the moon comes up?" Laura asked.

"Not tonight. Your mama and I have to talk." That was the signal that it was bedtime. "Get some sleep.

Some of you will be leaving for Aunt Dora's in the morning. Annie, get."

Annie moved—not very fast—into the kitchen, and stood in the shadows behind the flour barrel.

When everybody went upstairs, it seemed quiet. Even the boys settled down fast. She kept still, hoping she'd get a chance to put real chips in the pan full of dirt. Then Jennifer came to the stairs.

"Annie."

She didn't answer.

"Annie! Where are you, Annie? Come on. Papa said bedtime."

She didn't have a choice.

"Annie, you're just acting naughty. Come here this instant."

"I'm coming."

She pretended to go to bed. She took off her dress and got into her nightshirt and crawled under the covers in her cot. Laura and Jennifer both slept in the big bed with Till.

Till had turned her back to the wall and buried her face in her pillow. Annie didn't even breathe while she listened to see if she could hear Mama and Papa talking. She would have to wait to go to bed until they moved away from the hearth. Till was still sobbing. Jennifer was trying to talk to her.

"He'll be back, Till. He loves you. If he gets a full-time job and sticks to it, and if he gets respectable, I think Papa will admire him and let him come back."

"I can't believe Papa said to pretend he's dead!" Till sobbed.

"You can see Rye and tell him you're sorry."

"Not if they make me go to Dora's tomorrow."

"You can write to him."

There was a minute of quiet.

"Maybe I will," Till whispered.

"Sure." Jennifer turned and talked so softly that Annie could not hear her. Her eyes began to feel heavy, but she rolled out of bed and started to the stairway.

"Is that you, Annie" Laura whispered. "What you doing?"

Her heart jumped up in her mouth. "Nothing."

"Where you going?"

"To the privy."

"Well, hurry it up," Laura whispered. "Honestly!"

"I'm hurrying."

She could hear no sound in the room off the parlor where Mama and Papa were sleeping. But when she walked as still as she could around the corner to the hearth, Mama heard her.

"Who is it? Annie, that you? Where you going?"

At that moment, when she reached the hearth, the moonlight was so bright she could see through the door that Mama turned her face toward her.

"Can I go to the privy?" Annie stammered.

Mama sighed. "Well, yes, Annie. But hurry it up. You ought to have taken care of that an hour ago."

Then Mama turned her head away. Annie backed up and lifted the dirt pan off the hearth. It was so heavy she stumbled a few steps to catch her balance.

"What are you doing, Annie?"

She didn't answer. She staggered as fast as she could under the load of dirt as she walked through the kitchen and out into the backyard. Under the full moon, she could see where she was going. She emptied the dirt out of the pan and started to work. The little chips of wood pricked and cut her fingers when she scooped them up off the ground in handfuls.

3

*S*uddenly Elizabeth Ann heard a clatter. She had been dozing. She looked up, thinking she had dropped those chips on the hearth. But her daughter Clara had just yanked up the window shade. Light flooded into the room. She thought she saw several more white-robed figures in the distance, but none of them looked familiar.

"I'm sorry I'm so noisy, Mama. Are you all right?" her daughter whispered.

"I'm all right," Elizabeth Ann said, her mouth dry. Clara gave her a drink with a straw.

"Remember I told you about my cousins Katy and Pauline Hunter?" Elizabeth Ann murmured.

"Yes," Clara said, taking the empty water glass.

"I was just thinking . . ." Her words were slow. "I wouldn't know them if I saw them now."

"No. Probably not." Clara breathed softly.

So Papa had told Till to pretend that Rye was dead. How could he have said that? Annie had seen possums, calves, and spiders dead. But she had never seen a person dead. She couldn't imagine that Papa had said "dead" about Rye. But he had said it. And she couldn't forget it.

But even these fretful thoughts couldn't dampen her excitement about going to Aunt Dora's. Her mind churned with anticipation, though she felt awkward being so cheerful while Till was so glum. When she looked out from her tiny window into the yard below, she saw her big sister standing near the horses, her red face swollen, a damp handkerchief knotted in her hands.

On the entire horseback ride to Aunt Dora's—Till and Farrell on one horse, Annie holding fast to Mama's waist on the other—Till had been mostly quiet, speaking only a sharp word now and then. Before they left, John and Papa had tied Katy's big present from the attic to Till's mare. Till was clearly unhappy about that, the big package bobbing against the side of the horse. Annie was sure the other package in the attic must be for her. Her fifth birthday was coming soon, and she was more than curious. Now when Katy opened the bundle, both of them would know what it was!

As they came upon the grassy meadow before the little farm laid out at the foot of the hills, Annie thought the pasture and trees looked like the mysterious inky drawings in a book she had seen at her Aunt Celia's house in Fillmore, called *Paradise Lost*.

Aunt Dora rushed out of the doorway toward them. Her shoulders seemed stooped as she ran. When she reached them, they could see that she had been crying.

"Dora!" Mama dismounted with Annie. "Dora, what is it?"

"Oh, I'm so glad to see you!" Aunt Dora fell into Mama's arms and rested her head on Mama's shoulder.

"What is it?"

Tears started to come up in Aunt Dora's eyes. Her hair was stringy around her tired face. "It's Katy," Aunt Dora breathed hard. "It's Katy, Helen. Katy's been taken with a terrible fever." Suddenly Aunt Dora clutched Mama's arms tightly. Then she leaned up toward Mama's ear and said something Annie could not hear.

"Oh, no," Mama breathed. "Stay outside, children. Your little cousin Katy is sick."

Annie didn't know what to think. Aunt Dora's other children had died from sickness. Till looked grim, as though she didn't want to be here at all, especially not now. But she handed Farrell down to Mama and slipped down from the saddle.

The grass in Aunt Dora's meadow was deep and dark, almost blue. With white daisies spotting it, it looked like Mama's navy polka-dot gingham.

Annie wondered how sick Katy was. She led one of the horses, Boots, up to the house, and Till took Old Brownie. "Are we going to give Katy her present?" Annie asked. Till was quiet, and Mama didn't answer.

By the time they reached the corral, Uncle Al was standing in the doorway, and Pauline was coming out to meet them. Jeremy Hunter came up from the barnyard to help tie up Boots.

"Well, are we?" she asked Till again.

"Shhh," Till whispered. "Katy has diphtheria."

Jeremy unpacked the horses and tended to them. Till and Farrell looked on quietly. Annie did not dare ask Till about Katy's birthday present again.

Finally Jeremy finished and handed them their bags. "Go up the back stairs and don't go near the front bedroom," he said quietly.

Pauline beckoned them through the barn door. "This way. I'll take you." Pauline, tall and slender beneath her bright gold hair, had freckles spattered across her nose. Everybody was quiet as they filed through the vegetable garden into the back door and up the steep stairway. "Put your bags here and then we'll go down to supper," Pauline told them. On her way downstairs to eat, Annie noticed Uncle Al standing by the front room window, his back to them and his hands in his pockets. Mama and Aunt Dora came through the half-open door of the front bedroom. Annie could see little Katy lying stone still, her head on a white pillow propped up against the dark headboard of Aunt Dora's big bed. Dinner was quiet. Annie was afraid to talk or to ask any questions.

It was still a quiet house when morning came. From Annie's chair at the round breakfast table, she could see Aunt Dora's fancy clock on the top of her French cupboard. Uncle Al and Aunt Dora had been able to bring with them their good things from Salt Lake City. The round clock face had marble pillars on each side of it. Gold leaves wound around the pillars. Mama said the leaves were covered with real gold.

"Eat your oatmeal, Annie!"

Mama seemed nervous, and Aunt Dora seemed nervous. Both of them had stayed up in the night with Katy. Till was up there with her, still.

Annie could barely pick up the heavy silverware Aunt Dora set at her table. Big silver roses curved along the handle of her spoon. Rather than lift the silverware, she ate the hot biscuits. They were delicious.

Finally, as they were eating, Till came down the stairs. Everyone was quiet watching her. She looked tense as she pushed a lock of hair out of her eyes. She didn't even say good morning. The first words she spoke were about Katy. "Katy wants some little birds' eggs to play with," she said.

Aunt Dora couldn't sit still at the table. She was walking about nervously, serving food, picking up the empty dishes. "More biscuits, Helen?" she asked.

"No, thank you," Mama said.

"It's all she can think about," Till said, "so I told her somebody might go to find some for her." Till was very pale, and her eyes looked as though she had been crying.

Aunt Dora was a big woman with large hands and thick wrists. It was strange that her children grew to be so small and thin. She still walked about nervously as though everything were different all at once.

"I'll go." Pauline wiped her mouth with her napkin and laid it beside her plate. Then she moved her chair back to get up.

But Aunt Dora didn't want her to go. "Oh no you don't!" she said. "Finish your oatmeal, girl."

"Can I go too?" Farrell cried. From where Annie sat she could see Farrell's head over the tablecloth and that was all. When his chin waggled, it seemed to touch the white lace. "Can I go? Please, Mama," he cried out again.

"I don't want anybody to go," Aunt Dora said. When she took the dishes up off the tablecloth her hands shook. "Percy was about Farrell's age when he slipped and fell last summer." Aunt Dora glanced at her last boy, Jeremy, who was busy chewing a piece of biscuit covered with Mama's blackberry jam. Once she had several boys. Now just Jeremy. "Jeremy would go. But he's got chores."

"Is Katy asleep?" Pauline asked Till.

"Yes, she's asleep now," Till said.

"Can't I go now?" Pauline asked, stuffing her cereal into her mouth and swallowing it.

"Can I go too? Please, Mama," Farrell begged.

Mama looked at Annie. She didn't need to ask;

she knew Annie wanted to go.

Annie jumped out of her chair so fast she almost took the tablecloth and china dishes with her.

"I'll go, Mama," she said quickly through a mouthful of biscuit.

Pauline motioned with her hand. "Come on, Annie," she said. "I'll show you." To her mother she said, "It won't hurt me just to let them see, Mama."

Aunt Dora looked after them, weary of arguing. She pushed the gray hair out of her eyes.

Farrell and Annie followed Pauline out into the vegetable garden and down a grassy slope to the spring. Clear, cold water bubbled out of the mountains and down through the meadow over a heap of moss-covered stones.

Pauline helped them jump across at a narrow place, and they began climbing up the canyon behind the house. The canyon was narrow, opening up in a few places just wide enough for the stream to flood into ponds where the beavers built their dams. The water skimmers clustered along the edges and scattered across the surface to the waterfalls. The deep leaves were moist and dark.

"Now, Mama doesn't want us going far," Pauline cautioned, "and there's a nest I know of close to here. Up . . ." She set her feet at an angle on the steep hillside.

"Where are you going?" Annie asked.

"Way up there. Can you see?" She pointed to a cliff. Farrell wanted to follow her. "But don't let Farrell come," Pauline cried. "You two stay right down there and watch." She wagged her finger like Mama often did.

Annie had to grab hold of Farrell's pants to keep him from going. Both of them watched Pauline mount the steep sandy hillside. As she climbed, she reached out to grasp little clumps of brush and trees.

"There's a nest on a limb over there," she called back to them, pointing to a half-dead gnarled tree at the foot of the sandstone cliff. It looked like she was going to climb the rocky cliff behind the tree to try to reach into the top branches.

Farrell and Annie watched, not breathing. Pauline stumbled on her skirt as she scrambled onto the rough rocks and climbed up over the embankment. She was very close to the edge. The cliff was much taller than the tree and straight up and down—like a wall. Only a few scrawny bushes jutted out from its sheer drop.

Pauline was brave. Annie could see she was going to walk out on a narrow shelf until she reached the top of the tree only a few feet away. They held their breath.

"I got them! I got them!" Pauline called when she reached the tree. She stopped on the shelf and slowly reached into a cranny far above. She placed something in the pocket of her apron: one, two, three times.

"There are three!" Pauline cried, turning and inching along the narrow shelf away from the tree. "There were three of them. I knew there would be . . ."

But she didn't finish. Suddenly she screamed. A blur of ruffled petticoats bounced and ripped and tore through the scraps of brush growing along the side of the steep sandstone.

Annie stood still. When Pauline stopped falling, she was hanging from a bush growing out of the rocks. One of her black slippers was caught against a crack just large enough for her to get a foothold. The other foot was swinging out over the cliff.

"Run, Annie! Run get Mother. I need help!" Pauline called.

Annie grabbed Farrell's hand, but he began to cry.
"Leave Farrell here," Pauline called. "Hurry!"

So Annie began to run.

"Mother . . . Mama! Help. I'm falling!" Pauline's voice filled the canyon with a frightening echo. Once or twice Annie stumbled, and fell, catching her foot on a root springing out of the ground. But she picked herself up and ran as fast as she could. The house was not far away. She could see it through the trees.

Aunt Dora must have seen her coming. She started running over the grassy slope, catching her apron and her skirts with both hands. "My land, Annie. My land! What is it?"

"Pauline's falling!" Her eyes ached from tears that wanted to come but couldn't.

"Oh, no!" Aunt Dora cried out, running very fast. Behind her came Till, running, stumbling, her long hair streaming behind her.

Annie could see Mama in the doorway. Mama had said she would stay and watch Katy. Uncle Al and Jeremy were with the sheep.

"No!" Aunt Dora panted, already out of breath.

They ran past the pond and up through the leaves. Finally they could see cousin Pauline twenty feet above them, her arms clutching the bush. Now both of her feet were hanging and she was sobbing hysterically. Aunt Dora tripped and stumbled over the rocks, trying to climb as close to Pauline as she could.

"Hang on, honey. Hang on, I'm coming!" Aunt Dora called with a sob in her throat. "Hang on, Pauline."

Aunt Dora began to climb the large boulders that mounted up the side of the cliff. Just as she pulled herself up on the first one, Pauline's hand slipped off the branches above her. She screamed as she fell.

Then she lay quiet over some jagged rocks at the foot of the sandstone cliff.

Aunt Dora screamed as she frantically stumbled over the stones.

It took a while for help to come. Finally Aunt Dora, Mama, and Till carried Pauline to the sofa, then spread her out straight and covered her up with thick blankets. Mama rushed to the kitchen and pumped up some cool water. Then she rubbed Pauline's face with a wet cloth. Till couldn't stop sobbing, with a sad wail that seemed weighted with all of her troubles.

Aunt Dora got down to business fast. "Jeremy, go down the road and fetch Mrs. Kelly. She'll know what to do. Till, go find Al in the field. Tell him what's happened. He's only down the meadow a piece." She sagged onto a chair. "Oh, Helen, I'm so afraid."

Mama carefully touched Pauline's thin arms. Farrell said, "There are some birds' eggs in her pocket."

While Mama smoothed Pauline's arms, Farrell lifted the blanket and tugged at Pauline's apron.

"Here, you," Mama spoke harshly. "Don't bother Pauline." But she lifted the blanket herself and found Pauline's apron pocket. Inside were the smashed shells.

"Wasted," Mama sighed. When Farrell took out a bit of shell and wiped it clean with the corner of his jacket, she said, "Throw it away, Farrell."

"But it's pretty, Mama." He tucked it in his pocket.

"It's a shame," Mama said. "All that's come of what could have been birds—or something to make Katy happy—now just a mess."

Aunt Dora picked up the apron to go with it into the kitchen. "Well, at least Pauline tried to please Katy. That's worth something." As she turned away, she took a handkerchief and blew her nose.

When Mrs. Kelly came, she recommended hot and cold packs, and mustard. She didn't leave until dark. It seemed extra quiet and murky in the parlor after she had gone. Though Dora had lit the lamps, she kept their flames low. Uncle Al sat in his rocker reading his newspaper. The fire lit up the logs in the fireplace. Mama should have told Annie to go to bed and take Farrell, but no one noticed what time it was. Till stood at the window watching Mrs. Kelly ride away. Annie had seen her give Mrs. Kelly a letter to take to Liza Hamblin in Circleville. It might be addressed to Liza, but Annie knew what was inside of it: something for Rye. She wouldn't say anything to anybody, but she could guess, because Till and Jennifer had talked that night about writing letters. Till had begun to look a little better this afternoon—almost encouraged, as though she had been able to get away with something very smart.

As the evening progressed, Annie sat still in a corner beside the sofa and watched Pauline, her arms bound up between lengths of pine wrapped in linen. Her head lay stiff against the pillows on the sofa, her eyes round with a dull light. Annie thought and thought about all that had happened that day.

When Mama took Annie and Farrell by the hand to their beds on the floor in the top bedroom, Till followed them. The house was quiet except for the *creak, creak* of Uncle Al's rocker. Annie lay her head against the cool pillow on the floor. *Creak. Creak.* Uncle Al and Aunt Dora were going to stay up all night with both of their sick children.

"Mama?" Annie asked. "Is it fair that something is always wrong with Aunt Dora's children?"

"No, life isn't fair, Annie." Mama lowered her head. Then, as though she needed to hear it, she quoted one of her favorite scriptures. *"All these things shall give thee experience, and shall be for thy good."*

"It isn't good," Annie dared to disagree. "We came all this way to see Katy. So why can't we go in her room? You get to go in there."

"She is very sick, Annie. Grownups know a little better how to protect themselves against the diphtheria."

"Are we going to give Katy her present?" she asked.

Mama was quiet.

"Mama?" she finally asked, not sure Mama had heard her.

"Not until she's better, Annie," Mama said.

Annie turned her cheek against the cool pillow and watched the breeze tap the vines against the window and throw shadows into the moonlight. Then she slept. In the darkest part of the night a strange sound disturbed her. Just as plain as daylight there was a feathery music of voices outside the window. She did not know what it was. Then she heard somebody crying below. She listened for a long moment but heard nothing else and finally drifted back to sleep.

In the morning the vines brushed the window casing and woke her up. Mama was not in bed. Neither was Till. Farrell was still sleeping.

Suddenly Annie thought she heard a tapping sound outside the window. This time it was not the vine, but the distinct *clack clack clack* of a hammer against green wood. She raised herself up on her elbows to listen. For a while it stopped. Then again, *clack clack*. So she slipped out of bed and walked to the low window that looked out over the back vegetable garden. There was Uncle Al below her, his bald head glistening in the morning light. He had nails in his mouth and took them out one by one. Holding them carefully, he tapped them into the wood. Annie could see that he was making a wooden box about the size of Farrell.

"Mama," Farrell suddenly called out.

"Shhh. Mama is downstairs," Annie said. "We must be very quiet because Katy and Pauline are sick."

Although Dora and Mama were busy in the kitchen, they were unusually quiet. When Annie and Farrell reached the bottom of the stairs, Mama picked up Farrell and held him tight. "Darling," she said, "please take a nice big piece of bread and jam and go out into the yard." Then Mama looked up at Annie. "You, too, Annie. Please take your breakfast into the yard and stay out of the house this morning."

Till was standing by the stove boiling some rags, and Aunt Dora was at the washboard washing out some towels. Her straw-colored hair straggled around her face; her eyes were swollen and red.

"There now," Mama handed the children bread and jam and opened the screen door. "There now. Go play in the garden."

Out in the sunshine, the flies danced around the bread and jam and crawled on the children's arms and hands. Farrell and Annie, laughing and sputtering, shooed them away. In the corner of the yard Uncle Al kept pounding nails into the wood.

"What are you making, Uncle Al?" Annie asked.

"Good morning, Annie."

"A big box?" Farrell commented, running his finger smoothly along the outside edge. The pine was yellow and clean.

Uncle Al was quiet.

"Where did you get such pretty wood?" Annie asked cautiously.

Uncle Al stood back and put his hands on his

hips. "This was our new picket fence," he said.

"Are you building a box, Uncle Al?" Farrell asked.

Uncle Al looked at Farrell and then at Annie. "You kids been in the house yet?" His eyes narrowed above his reddened cheeks.

"Mama made us come outside," Annie said. "Why? What's going to happen?"

Uncle Al knelt down in the grass and circled Annie in one arm and Farrell in the other. He stayed kneeling and holding them close. "Didn't your mama tell you what happened?" He choked a little and held them close for a long time.

Farrell squirmed. But Annie stood quiet trying to be polite.

"The angels came last night," he said quietly. "Aunt Dora heard them singing."

"The angels?" Annie opened her eyes wide.

"They came to help Katy."

Angels in the night. The music Annie heard must have been the angels in the night coming to take Katy. That was the first time she had ever heard that angels came to sick people.

"I heard the angels, too," she said.

"You did?" Uncle All looked at her kindly.

She nodded. "Outside my window I heard the angels singing."

"The angels took Katy with them," Uncle Al said softly.

Annie was quiet. She thought about it. The angels had come to take Katy with them? As she thought about it, she stared into the woods ahead. Her eyes felt heavy and dry. Katy must be in heaven by now.

Leaving Till with Pauline, Uncle Al and Aunt Dora got the wagon ready to take Katy's box to the Hunter plot of the graveyard several miles away.

Annie and Farrell sat by Mama on the wagon seat. Annie held herself tight against the jarring, clattering motion of the wagon, and the rattle of the wooden box behind them. Her mother had let her watch from a distance while they dressed Katy in her best Sunday dress and lay her gently in that wooden box.

When they reached the burial hill, several others came to stand with the family. Uncle Al pulled the casket from the back of the wagon. Aunt Dora helped him lower it to the ground. Then she threw herself on it. "Katy, Katy," she cried.

Annie hurt inside. Part of Katy had gone to live with the angels. Part of her was pale and cold inside of that box. That is what it meant to die. They would not see the real Katy again until they sealed her up in the endowment house. Annie was not sure how that happened. All she knew was that Katy's body was somewhere deep inside of that box, and the box would go deep into the ground.

Where had Katy really gone? While the grown-ups held a meeting in the small church, Annie ran with Farrell into the meadow to catch butterflies, but she was soon tired and sad. She sat in the shade beside the stream and wove clover together while in her mind she saw Katy floating in her billowing night dress up into the sky with the angels. Yet somehow part of Katy was in the box that slid deep into the ground. She had become two Katys.

It was hot, and with the flies buzzing around her, Annie grew sleepy. Finally Uncle Al, Aunt Dora, and Mama were ready to ride in the wagon back to Aunt Dora's. It seemed like a long trip. Annie was tired, but kept her eyes open, fastened on the bright sky fading under the gathering clouds. Everything seemed like a dream. Her head felt empty as though all her thinking had floated away with the music she had heard in the night. She remembered yesterday and the day before, and faraway in her mind a thought crowded up that didn't seem to belong in this time or place, yet it kept pounding in her head. She remembered the bundle they had tied to old Brownie to give to Katy. She knew it was still in the barn. She couldn't stop thinking of the outline of the mysterious bundle when she saw the barn in the distance like a huge black rock nestled in the valley. She thought about Katy with the angels, perhaps weeping and reaching for her present. It hurt to know Katy would never touch it or open it. Her touching hands were buried deep, and the alive winging part of her would not be here again.

"Mama," she said sleepily. She was huddled close against her mother's waist, her head resting against her shawl. "When Katy is sealed, will she be together again?"

"What, Annie?

"Will her body have her alive part again?"

Mama brushed Annie's brow with her gloved hand, pulling the wisps of hair away from her eyes. "Yes, Annie. The real Katy will be together again."

The wagon jolted and rocked them all back and forth, back and forth. But the rattle of the wooden box was gone.

"It's a little like my glove. You see. When my hand is inside the glove, it can move. When I take my hand out of the glove, it cannot move anymore."

Mama replaced her glove and rubbed Annie's brow. Annie thought that probably "being sealed" meant the glove would be stuck with glue so it would never come off again, but she didn't want to say anymore. She wanted to go to sleep, but she felt Mama's hand tighten on her shoulder. When Annie looked ahead she could see the daisies waving and shimmering in the long meadow of shaggy grass. Aunt Dora leaned forward. A tiny distant figure ran toward them from the house. It was Till, her white sleeves rolled up to the elbows, her hair flying behind her in the wind.

"What is it?" Aunt Dora gasped.

"Mama! Aunt Dora!" Till stumbled toward them.

Uncle Al stopped the wagon. Dora screamed, then clapped her hands against her mouth.

"It's Pauline," Till cried, gasping and crying. "It's Pauline. She quit breathing, Mama. She isn't breathing. I can't make her breathe, Mama!"

Till climbed up into the wagon, her face streaming with tears. Mama rested Till's head against her shoulder and rocked her.

4

*E*lizabeth Ann had been dreaming again. She woke in a sweat. No one had said life or death would be easy. The summer that Katy and Pauline had left them had been her first experience with dying.

"Someone's here to see you, Mama." Some people had come to visit. Mr. and Mrs. Hammond and Maude Winslow. Elizabeth Ann smiled and turned to her friends when they touched her hand.

"When you see Geneva, tell her I raised Elba to be a fine girl," one of the ladies whispered.

My goodness. Would she be seeing Geneva, who had left some two years ago? "I will," Elizabeth Ann whispered. Yes, she would, in all probability, be seeing Katy and Pauline again, too. "I will," she repeated.

When her friends left, the room seemed empty. Things looked clearer than they had for a long time. She thought again about Katy, Pauline and Till. Till wasn't much good after that, Elizabeth Ann remembered. No one was. A part of them had truly gone somewhere else. And now, here she was, expecting she'd go there, too.

After Katy and Pauline had been buried, Papa let Till and Annie go home while Mama stayed with Farrell to help Aunt Dora. Papa still wouldn't let Till see Rye, but he knew they shouldn't stay at Aunt Dora's anymore.

"There's too much tragedy at that Hunter place," he said. He advised Aunt Dora and Uncle Al to leave, to farm in some other state—perhaps Idaho, where some of Uncle Al's people were. "There's not much left for you in Utah," Papa had told them. "Especially in that canyon." So Mama had stayed behind at the Hunters' to help them get ready to move to Idaho. Annie thought the house seemed quiet while Mama was gone—even though almost everyone was there. Papa didn't talk much. No one laughed very much. Till was unhappy—partly because she could not see Rye and partly because it had upset her so much when Katy and Pauline died. It upset everyone. Annie had never remembered such a quiet time.

When the weather got hot and sticky, she knew it was time for her birthday soon—August twenty-first. The time went by slowly. While everyone did their chores and played in the pastures, Annie kept watching Till post letters to Liza Hamblin. Soon, as mail trickled back, Till began to get fat letters. Annie knew they were letters from Rye. Annie knew, because she heard Till and Laura and Jennifer whispering and talking about it, and because John and Peter teased Till every chance they got. They shouted crazy verses that John made up.

Rye and Till
Rye and Till
If he don't kiss her
Nobody will.

Till shouted back, "It's none of your business!" Or, "Nothing's going on between us." In the evening as regularly as clockwork, Till went to the window to search the road for Rye, hoping he would come riding past the house on his way home from the mill. But he didn't come.

At noon, only a week before Annie's birthday, Till came from the post office with a letter. She was laughing and crying and laughing again.

"He's got a job in Fillmore! He's got a job in Fillmore!" she cried. "He's done it!" She ran out to the cow pasture waving the letter. "Papa!" Till screamed.

"Rye?" Papa said.

"He's working at Harper's Seed, Poultry and Implement Company in Fillmore," Till cried, half laughing. "See, . . . right here. It says."

For a moment Papa stopped and took the letter in his hands and held it away from his eyes the right distance. He read while everyone was quiet.

"Harper's Seed, Poultry and Implement. Well, I'll be blessed!" He looked the letter over. Then he glanced at Till, "You been corresponding with that young snip?"

Till looked down and didn't answer. Papa asked her again, and she swallowed hard.

"This letter is from Liza Hamblin, Papa. She lives close to him in Circleville and, well, she just tells me what Rye has been doing. Papa . . ." She tried to smile, but Papa's face was grim. She drew up, standing tall like Mama sometimes did. Her words were steady. "Papa, Rye has gone to Fillmore and got a job. Not just a part-time job at the mill but a job in a big town selling tools and seeds for a big company. He'll make plenty of money now. He'll show you he is a responsible person, Papa."

Laura, Peter, and Annie followed close on Papa's heels while he walked up to the house. He was awfully quiet. Everyone else was, too. Finally he took the letter between his finger and thumb and shook it.

"Well, that doesn't sound bad," he said.

Till's breath quickened. She clasped her hands. "Then you'll let me . . ."

"Wait a minute!" Papa said. He drew back and took a deep breath. "I didn't give permission for anything. He may have a job today and be out on his ear tomorrow." Papa handed the letter to Till. He started walking. "Give him a few weeks."

Till clutched the letter in her hand and stumbled over the grass. "Oh, Papa. He'll still be working next week. He'll work forever! I know it!"

"Give him a week," Papa repeated. "Inside of a week he'll be drunk in the street and wishing he was back part-time at the mill."

"Oh, no, Papa," Till protested. "He's decent now. Oh, Papa, he wants to do right." Till had tears in her eyes.

Annie could tell that Papa was surprised and a little bit pleased.

"Okay. But give him . . . a month," Papa said.

Till rushed ahead clasping the letter in her hands.

More than a week passed before Mama came back. Annie was happy to see her. Now they could make cheese and butter in their new kitchen. Papa had only a few more nails to pound and the windows to glue. It was a big kitchen with a good pine floor. Now they had five rooms: two on top, Mama and Papa's bedroom below on the south side, the main room, and now a new kitchen hooked on the back of the main room, big and roomy with wide windows. They ate their meals there now. Mama had a basin next to the pump and her stove right next to the cupboard.

"Get me some more salt from the barrel, Annie," she said.

When Annie returned carrying the pan filled with the crusty salt, Mama had just finished pounding a great gob of churned butter into the stone crock. She tapped it down to about an inch from the top and laid a white cloth over it. Then she poured the salt over the cloth and pounded it down level all over the top of the butter. When they put the crock in the cellar behind the house, the salt made the butter keep.

While Mama worked, Papa came in with nails in his mouth and got a bucketful of water to wash the paste off the windows.

Till had gone to the post office.

"Well, I don't know what to say to her about it," Papa said.

"It seems he's trying hard," Mama said while she was pushing on the salt.

"Maybe I'll get on to Fillmore on this next trip. I've been thinking about trading the mule." Papa spoke like he thought—often in disconnected sentences. "Got to take the wheat and wool to the mills at Kingston in a couple weeks. I'll go on to Fillmore—check to see if Rye really got a job there. I'll ask Matt Harper how the boy works. I'll get wind at the saloon if he's drinking much."

Mama looked at Annie quickly. "Shhh, John."

"What?" Papa asked. "I've got a right to check up on a man who may be my son-in-law." When he looked at Mama, she shook her head slightly with her eyebrows knit. He lowered his voice to a thin sound as though he were keeping a secret. "It's not the saloon you're worried about, is it, Mama?" He paused, then, struggling to make sense out of everything. "The past is the past, Helen," Papa said.

For a moment both Mama and Papa were quiet. The room felt strange. Then Mama turned. "I believe you, John."

Annie didn't understand what she meant. "Is Papa going all the way to Fillmore?" she asked.

Mama smiled. "Yes, I guess so, Annie."

Annie rushed over to Papa, who took the nails out of his mouth and put them in his pocket. He lifted the bucket of water and started for the door.

"Oh, Papa!" Annie cried. She didn't really need to tell him that she wanted to go with him to Fillmore, because he already knew.

"Well, let's see," Mama said. "Pretty soon it's your birthday!"

"All right," Papa said. "Let's say if you're especially good we'll take you to Fillmore as a birthday present."

For the next few weeks Annie tried to be better than just good. With Laura, Peter, and John, she walked into the hills picking bits of wool off the bushes and out of the fences where the sheep caught themselves when they walked by. At nights the family sat around the fire and picked over the wool until it was fluffy and soft and clean. Then Mama carded it into bats about eight or ten inches long and three inches wide. The bats looked like hair snarled and tossed into thin strips. She pressed the bats into long narrow rolls end to end to make thread. After she had single threads, she sat at the spinning wheel and wound three threads together into a good strong yarn. The children watched her while they picked at the wool. Sometimes she boiled the yarn in rabbit brush or onion peelings to make it yellow, or she used red onion skins to get red and copperas to get green.

When it came time for Annie's fifth birthday, Annie made sure everyone knew she hadn't touched the bundle in the closet. She had only opened the door once or twice and looked inside. Both bundles were still there. She wondered how Katy's bundle had come back from Uncle Al's barn in the canyon. She wanted to ask, but she wouldn't say anything until her birthday was over.

"You've been especially good, Annie," Mama said. "What special thing to eat would you like on your birthday?" Annie asked for an oatmeal cake, the kind Mama made with brown sugar.

Annie was still awake when Jennifer and Till came into the room and slipped into their bed by the window. They thought she was asleep. But Annie couldn't help but overhear what they were saying.

"I can't stop him, Jenny," Till whispered. "He won't stay away."

Annie knew they weren't talking about her birthday.

"It's been a whole month," Jennifer whispered.

"It'll be Annie's birthday, and Papa can't be upset."

Then Jennifer giggled and snuggled down in the covers next to the window. "I'm glad, Till," she whispered softly. Annie wondered what Jennifer was so glad about.

She woke up hearing her sister Laura snore from the big bed beside her. The rising sun glazed the room with brightness. She decided to dress before anybody else knew it was morning. But Mama was already separating the cream, and Papa and John were out in the barnyard emptying the slop bucket into the hog pen.

"Well, it's August twenty-first today!" Mama smiled. "Just five years ago today Annie was born into this world!" Mama leaned close to Annie and folded her in her arms. Annie hung on her neck and smelled the sweet smell of flour and soda. "It's so nice to have you, Annie. Even if you've been a little trouble now and then. Even if we don't have any apples from the tree to make pie this year." She put Annie down and kissed her once more on the cheek.

It seemed like forever before they dried all the dishes and took down the cake pans to start the oatmeal batter for the birthday cake. Mama put big hunks of butter and brown sugar and oatmeal and eggs and milk into the bowl.

In the afternoon Mama had everyone gather green beans from the garden. Laura and Farrell and Annie snapped them into a pan and washed them at the pump. They picked off some ears of corn, tore off the husks, and put them into the biggest kettle they had. Mama didn't put them on the fire until almost everything else was ready.

At four o'clock Papa came in with John and Peter from gathering up the sheep. Tomorrow the hired men would come in from Circleville and begin the shearing. The wheat and wool would be ready to take to the mills by the first of September.

Papa was in a good mood. "We got all the sheep, Mama!" he said cheerfully, tossing his gloves on the table. "Not even one is lost! Isn't that almost unbelievable!"

"It is!" Mama said. Most of the time some of the sheep got lost—just like some people, Papa had always said. "What a good thing to happen on Annie's birthday!"

Papa stopped and looked at Annie in her best starched pinafore. She clutched her hands tightly behind her back.

"Well, blessed if it ain't so! Annie's birthday today! Five years old. How do you like that!" He swooped down and lifted her up into his arms until she could see over his dark, shiny hair.

"A big girl now," he laughed. He hugged her and whirled her until she giggled.

"Get yourself washed," Mama said. "We're about to have a big supper. Laura, tell Jennifer and Till to come in from the quilt."

"And where's Annie's big surprise we've been waiting to open?" Papa said. Annie's heart raced. Would she really get to take that present out of the sack and the straw? "Run up and get it, John, and let's have a real birthday party."

When the package came down the stairs on John's back, she couldn't help herself from crying out. She was still trying to be good enough to go with Papa to Fillmore, so she put her hand over her mouth.

John laid the bundle under the buffet in the main room, and everyone gathered around the big table in the kitchen, set with Mama's best lace cloth and a vase full of summer leaves.

They knelt at their chairs while Papa prayed in a very deep, gentle voice. "And thank you, God, for sending Annie. It's good to have her in our house. In the name of Jesus Christ, amen."

Mama looked at Annie, smiling, while everyone got into their chairs around the table and began passing around the beans, the pork, and the corn and biscuits. Annie felt very important, but she had a hard time eating anything. She could see the bundle on its side under the china cupboard. Till was sitting quietly in front of it, hiding it with her skirt.

"We'll have the wool and the wheat ready to take to the mills in a week, then," Papa announced. "Now just how many blankets do you want and how much flannel to sew up the clothes, Helen?"

Annie was too excited to pay attention.

When all the food was eaten, John said, "Now let's have Annie open her bundle and Mama bring in the cake."

Annie squeezed her hands together under the tablecloth.

"Just hold your horses," Mama said. She and Jennifer and Till began taking the dishes away. When Till got up, her skirts brushed away and Annie could see the gift. John put it beside her chair and started to cut the binding thread with his pocket knife.

"Let Annie open it!" Peter shouted.

It wasn't Christmas, but it was like Christmas.

"Here, here. No package is worth quarreling about," Papa said, and helped to pull the thread away. Straw poked up through the opening of the sack.

"Pull the sack away, Annie," Peter said, and she pulled. Down came the straw and the sack. Her heart pumped hard. She saw a little piece of wood about the size of the seat in a swing, painted black with delicate red and yellow flowers and green leaves on it. And down from the wood were little spokes like the legs on Mama's china cart. It was the back of a chair just big enough for her to sit in!

"It's a chair! It's a chair, Mama!" she shouted, pulling away the straw and tugging at the burlap.

"A special kind of chair," Papa said.

She wondered what those rounded wooden shapes

were when she had felt them in the clothes closet. Now she could see the bows painted with red and yellow flowers curving up past the ends of the four small legs. "It's a rocking chair, Papa!" she shouted, throwing her arms around his neck.

The little chair rocked back and forth, back and forth.

"Thank you, Papa," she cried. Then she remembered that the other package was to belong to Katy. For a moment she was sad. "Is Katy's package a chair?" she asked.

Papa hugged her close and kissed her hair. He didn't talk right away. "Those two little chairs were to give you two little girls a good start rocking through your lifetimes." He paused. "Think you can rock enough for two, Annie?"

Before she could answer, Mama brought in the cake and everybody sang happy birthday. Next to Christmas, this should be the happiest day ever. And it was. But still, Annie couldn't help thinking about Katy.

"But Katy's chair . . . she can't rock. . . ."

"Please don't worry about Katy. She and Pauline are happy where they are," Mama said. "Katy has changed. But you'll change, too. Worry about Annie."

Just as they finished their oatmeal cake Till jumped up and ran to the window.

"It's him! Oh, Papa, I couldn't stop him. . . ."

"What?" Papa jumped up and rushed to the window. "Well, I'll be doggoned!" he exclaimed, wadding up his napkin. "If it isn't your Rye Hadley looking dapper on a smart mare! Come clean from Fillmore!"

Till turned and ran to Mama. "Mama . . . I couldn't stop him. He said if Papa'd give him one month, he'd give Papa one month. He said he was coming in from

Fillmore in one month, and I couldn't do anything about it."

Rye Hadley looked spanking clean, his dark blond hair smooth and washed and thick. He got off his mare like he owned the place and came walking up to the door. Papa strode to the door and opened it. "Well, I'll be doggoned. What do you think you're doing here this time of the day, Rye Hadley?"

Rye walked in, his bright blue eyes shining. "I've come for Clothilda."

Till was standing beside Mama, her cheeks flushed and her hair mussed around her face. She looked beautiful.

"It's about time I got permission to marry your daughter, Mr. Wood. I'm tired of waiting!"

Till ran into Rye's arms and pressed her head against his cheek.

"I figured you'd be proud I got me a full-time job in Fillmore, and I got wind you was going to give me about a month. Well, a month is gone, and I'm still working and doing well." Rye Hadley held Till in the circle of his arm.

"Well, I'll be," Papa exclaimed.

"Well?" Rye Hadley spoke up with a strong voice.

Papa looked at Rye and then Till and then Mama. "Well," Papa stroked his chin. "This is unexpected. And sudden!"

"We'll wait until Christmas, Papa," Till said softly. "Be we want to know. . . ."

"We deserve to know," Rye spoke up again. "This isn't nothing sudden, not really."

Papa had to agree. "Well, I guess you're right. And I suppose I expected it."

All of them were watching and holding their

breaths. Mama wiped her cheek.

"Well?" said Rye.

"Well . . ." Papa walked away a little bit, knitting his brow and hitting the napkin against the leg of his britches. "Well . . . I'd just as soon she married a bear." He looked up at Mama. "You're so doggoned romantic-minded. You women. All feelings and no reason."

Everyone was silent but Till. "Does that mean yes, Papa? Oh, Papa!" She rushed up to Papa and stood right in front of him, watching him close and clasping her hands. "Papa. . . ?"

"There's no stopping you, is there?" Papa said slowly. "But I'd just as soon you married a bear."

Till didn't seem to hear anything about the bear. "Oh, Papa, thank you!" Papa backed away trying not to lose his balance.

Till ran to Rye Hadley and kissed him hard on the mouth.

Jennifer and Laura and Mama stood together, laughing and crying all at the same time. John and Peter shouted and danced. Annie sat down in her new chair.

5

Elizabeth Ann was remembering the chair at the same time she was looking at it in front of her eyes with her little granddaughter in it. Long ago when it had needed painting, Elizabeth Ann had painted it yellow. It was yellow now.

"Robin!" Clara's voice came from the kitchen over the warm smell of baking bread.

Sitting in Annie's rocker, Robin looked bright and cheerful in the light of the Christmas tree in the corner of the room. She was rocking back and forth, back and forth in the little yellow chair while it creaked with that familiar sound. Clara, her mother, had rocked in that same chair when she was a little girl.

"Grandma's sleeping!" someone whispered. Elizabeth Ann could hear Clara come into the room.

"I'm not sleeping," Elizabeth Ann said. "I'm fine. Seems I'm getting ready for that long trip I'm going to take, and that it's going to take place around Christmastime."

"Mama, you promised," Clara began. "Not until after Christmas! Can't you just visit with some friends this afternoon?"

"I'm not going anywhere yet," Elizabeth Ann said. "But I don't need that little chair around here anymore. It's time for Robin to take the chair. It's hers now. I'm finished with my rocking." She vaguely heard the runners scrape the rug as Clara dragged it into the hallway.

Now Elizabeth Ann returned to imagining her papa. It was just as if he stood there in the room.

Papa was going to Fillmore to sell the mule. But everyone knew he was also going to check up on Rye Hadley.

Until it was time to go on the exciting trip to Fillmore, Annie sat inside the upstairs closet in her rocker, looking out on the wet meadow through the chinks in the wood. The day was quiet and cloudy, but the light coming from under the roof was enough to help her pick the burrs and grass out of the wool she had gathered. She was making Till a blanket for her wedding. She hoped Mama would make it into yarn for her. But she wouldn't tell what she was going to do with it. Then she would ask Aunt Celia in Fillmore to show her how to use her knitting needles. Till would be so proud of her. It would be a surprise because she would knit it here inside of the closet, sitting in her rocker.

Now that the rain didn't patter so hard on the roof, she could hear sounds from the barnyard. Papa and one of the sheep shearers stepped outside the barn and held their hands out to see how much it was raining. The sheep huddled together to keep warm now that their wool was gone. It was lucky Papa and the men finished the shearing yesterday before the wool got wet. Now Annie could hear them getting ready to bag it and carry the bags out to the wagon. It would be supper soon. Annie went downstairs.

"You think it's going to stop raining?" Mr. Hamblin wondered aloud. Every year he came from Circleville with Liza for the shearing. But Liza hadn't come this time. Instead Mr. Hamblin brought Caleb, who was Laura's age. He was a big boy, bigger than

John, with dark red hair curled tight on his neck. He had enormous hands spattered with brown freckles, and he had a habit of staring at people. He came to dinner with the rest of the men.

There were two or three hired men from the Order at Circleville who helped Papa with the shearing. Caleb was big enough to be counted as one man, and Mr. Fergusson was the name of the other. With all three sitting at the dinner table with the family, it made a crowd. Mama and the girls had to fix heaps of potatoes and whole potfuls of gravy.

Caleb Hamblin ate with his spoon in his hand like a shovel. Between mouthfuls he said, "Pass the bread."

"How much bread, a whole loaf?" John said.

Laura, Jennifer, and Peter looked up and then laughed.

Caleb laughed with them. "You think I eat big. There's somebody eats even more'n me. It's Rye Hadley."

"Rye Hadley?" Laura asked.

"You seen Rye Hadley?" Jennifer asked.

"At home. Eats all of us poor."

Till was serving corn on the cob. She straightened up her back when they began talking about Rye.

"He's a sly one. Takes advantage of you every time," Caleb managed to laugh while he was chewing.

Till could not stand by in silence. "Well, he has got a full-time job at the Harper Seed P and I," she emphasized.

"Yeah, as if that amounts to anything," Caleb grinned, still chomping on his potatoes.

"Then what's funny?" Laura demanded.

Caleb chewed a minute, then washed everything down with a gulp of milk. "It's funny old Till here thinks she's going to marry that smart aleck Rye Hadley."

Till frowned and put down her fork. "What's got into you, Caleb Hamblin?"

"Oh, never mind!" Caleb turned away, and snickered behind his hand. He filled his mouth full of bread and his big jaw went up and down.

"No, what is it?" Peter demanded.

Annie was sitting between Till and Laura, and Caleb was sitting across from them at the long kitchen table. The grownups at the other end ignored them. Till pretended that she didn't care. She leaned over to help Annie cut up her meat.

"Rye Hadley is sweet on my sister Liza!" Caleb laughed.

Till looked up slowly. "Oh, silly," she scoffed. "Liza has been writing to me about Rye."

"He was over to our house all the time while he was still living in Circleville," Caleb grinned. "And Liza is going to be in Fillmore this fall to go to school! They're mighty close for just friends."

Till looked startled. "You're the one who doesn't know what's going on, Caleb Hamblin. And I wish you'd keep your nose out of other people's business."

Jennifer looked up, surprised. But Till went on. "Liza helps me know what's going on, and she will continue to inform me in the fall. I know she's going to be in Fillmore. Rye has been giving Liza his letters to send to *me*." She pointed at herself. "Me, me, me."

"*Me, me, me*," Caleb imitated in a high-pitched voice.

"You're just sickening, Caleb," Laura said and turned away to the others who also seemed upset by the conversation. "Please pass the butter."

Caleb gobbled up another mouthful of potatoes, and nobody said anymore. But Till was upset, Annie could tell. Deep color was rising under her hair just behind her ear lobes, and she put down her fork and didn't eat anymore.

The family gladly watched the men from Circleville go when the shearing was done. "That Caleb is the kind to eat a body out of house and home." Mama shook her head.

On the morning of Papa's trip to Fillmore it stopped raining. Annie was impatient watching Pa and the boys load up the bags of wool and grain to take to the mills in Kingston. It was eleven o'clock in the morning before they got to the mills, said hello to Papa's brothers who were in charge, and left their load. When the brothers were finished hauling, they stood around the sway-backed mule, speculating how much money Papa could get for such an animal. Finally, when they had all determined what Papa should ask, they waved to Annie perched high on the wagon. She set her skirts right and waited for Papa to drive her to Fillmore.

It was northwest a few miles to Circleville, but then due north on a longer road to Fillmore. As they began the journey, her throat was dry with excitement. It would take two days. They would stay the first night at Cove Fort and the next night at Aunt Celia's. The weather was good. All the wheat fields looked clean, rolling into the distant flannel hills. The sky was bright blue.

Papa was tall. When he sat on the wagon seat, his head rode above the mountains. He had dark thick hair, now growing gray close to his ears. A bushy mustache hung over the edges of his chin and covered his mouth. The hairs bobbed when he talked. His eyes were deep blue, set back beneath his thick eyebrows. His long nose jutted out straight, and two deep lines ran from his nose to his jaw.

He held the reins lightly as he rested his big hands on his knee. There was old grease and black dirt all around the edges of his round flat fingernails. Annie no longer noticed the countryside as she studied Papa's big hands.

This was the first chance she had ever had to be with her papa alone. He didn't say much unless she asked questions. And even then, sometimes he didn't answer her.

"Just exactly where is Katy?" she had asked earlier.

"In heaven."

"Where's heaven?"

"Up. Somewhere. Jesus is taking care of her. Don't worry about Katy."

"Will God be there with Katy, too?"

"Yes, Heavenly Father will be with Katy, too. Everyone, even people who make mistakes, will go to heaven, unless they are very bad."

"Is Rye bad?"

Papa didn't answer that question. So she asked another question about Rye. About what he was going to be when he grew up.

"That young fellow won't live to grow up at all if he don't learn to conduct himself proper," Papa said sharply. She didn't press him further.

It seemed to be a long time before Papa resumed his friendly talk after that. They ate their evening picnic in the wagon—sandwiches and Mama's raspberry popovers. Then Papa began singing in a deep bass voice that seemed to echo under the sky,

> *Tom Bolyn had no britches to wear.*
> *He bought him a sheepskin and made him a pair.*
> *The woolly side out and the skinner side in,*
> *They'll be cool in the summer, said Tom Bolyn.*

Cove Fort was just a big stone wall as far as Annie could tell. When the sky began to fade out she could see the inside of the buildings lit from within by candlelight. When it grew darker and cooler, they pulled the wagon inside the big wooden fort gate, and Papa parked it where it would be safe from any animals that wanted to raid their lunch box. People from the fort came to talk to Papa, and it was a while before he was ready to settle down for the night. When they were alone together, Annie asked him to tell her a story.

"Well, Annie. Here's the place that could tell you many a tale. It's here the unfriendly Indians got into the fort one night when the men were gone. The women and children were scared, but your grandma took care of everybody. She had the gift of tongues. When all those Indians rode right into the fort on their ponies, she began to sing, *Stop and Tell Me, Red Man*. And the Indians understood what she was singing."

Papa spread out their blankets. It was getting cold, and Annie was tired. They didn't bother to get out of their clothes.

"Your grandma was a great woman—a true pioneer," he whispered softly. "You can imagine that everybody was pretty scared of those Indians. Probably not a soul moved a muscle. Everybody was waiting to see what the Indians would do, and then your grandma started singing high and sweet at the top of her voice with the gift of tongues. The Indians' faces changed, and they skedaddled through that fort gate faster than a man could say, *Hey Joe.*"

Papa looked around in the darkness. Only a few lamps flickered in the houses at the other end of the fort. A gray stretch of clouds hung like a curtain behind the black wall.

Papa said it was time for prayers, so Annie rose to her knees, trying to keep the blankets from slipping off her shoulders. "Dear Father, our God." Papa talked as though he were speaking to a friend. "We thank thee for coming this far with us and hope you'll keep us company the rest of the journey."

It was such a long prayer that it was hard for Annie to concentrate. Instead, she worried about the blanket. If it slipped, would she dare pull it up risking the fury of Papa, or God, who seemed very close in this night with only the stars and moon between them and the place called heaven?

After a long list of thank yous, Papa asked a long list of blessings. He believed in covering everything. "And help us get a good price for the mule, if it be thy will. Amen."

After the prayer, she knew Papa had been talking with somebody he respected very much. "For all our falling short, the Lord still loves us and counts us his friends," Papa said. Annie stayed quiet. "We mustn't forget, Annie. The Lord is our best friend. And sometimes our only friend. Remember that he always stays by us."

"I won't forget." she promised.

She thought she could hear her words flying like birds' wings into the night.

6

*F*illmore, Deseret's first capitol city, was the biggest town Annie had ever seen. Large stores and buildings lined both sides of Main Street. The big houses in the residential areas were decorated with fancy woodwork. Aunt Celia, Papa's sister, lived with Uncle Dan and their children in one of the tallest adobe houses. The shutters were painted white, and a rambling front porch spread from one end of the house to the other. Only one window stood on each side of the big front door. The curtains were pulled back from the window on the right, and Annie could see faces watching them—Eva, who was Annie's age, and little Bertha. None of the older boys—Ed, George, Frank, or Culbert—were there.

Papa lifted Annie down and gave her the patchwork night bag. Aunt Celia opened the big front door and quietly waited, smiling. When Annie stepped into Aunt Celia's warm house, the hazy morning seemed to dissolve behind her. The front room was crowded with colored rugs, afghans, and stuffed chairs.

"Little Elizabeth Ann Wood! I'm so glad to see you!" Aunt Celia looked the same as Annie remembered her about a year back when she had come to Coyote. She was gentle and had read in her soft voice out of the big book, *Paradise Lost*. Annie hoped she could hear the story again and get a better look at the strange and beautiful inky drawings of Adam and Eve gazing at the flowers and trees in the Garden of Eden.

My, how you have grown!" Aunt Celia leaned her face close to Annie's cheek and squeezed her shoulders. Annie returned a half kiss in her aunt's hair. "Land sakes, John Wood, you have a charmer in this little daughter. I'm so glad you could come early enough for a good breakfast."

"My mouth is watering for some of your sourdough griddle cakes," Papa grinned, his hands in his pants pockets.

Papa and Annie followed Aunt Celia through the kitchen to the back of the house into a big enclosed room that looked like it had once been a back porch. Eva showed Annie where to hang her coat. Then she ran upstairs to find her doll while Annie found a place for her bag. Next to the porch wall there was a large bed covered with a blue quilt where Papa would sleep, and a small couch on the other wall where she would sleep. Near the back door there were shelves filled with books. Annie had never seen so many books in one place. She quickly looked for the book with the pictures of Adam and Eve. But it wasn't there.

"Just put your bags on the bed and hang your things on that hook by the side of the door," Aunt Celia called to Papa from the kitchen. "How is Helen? And how are the children?"

"Fine. Every one of them is fine. The children are growing like weeds."

"My, yes! And from the news I hear, that pretty eldest one of yours is about to be married."

"Till?" Papa hung up his coat and went to the kitchen door. "Ah, she just thinks she's going to get married. She's got a fellow—and she's hankering for him. Why, I don't know."

"She's getting to that ready age," Aunt Celia said. She probably noticed that Papa was a bit edgy.

"Yes, well, she's getting to that age, all right. Old enough to want her way, yet still too young to know what's best for her." He paused for a long time. "You know anything about any new young fellow in town—just got a job at the Harper Seed P and I? His name is Rye Hadley."

Aunt Celia took her spoon halfway out of the sourdough pancake batter. "Hmmmm. Rye Hadley. Harper Seed?" Both Papa and Annie waited. "Well, yes. I have seen a new young man at the seed company, and he's a good-looking young man at that. Do you mean to say he's the fellow Till has set her heart on?"

Papa's eyes flashed. "Do you know anything else about him?" he questioned.

Aunt Celia hesitated. She popped the pancake batter on the griddle, looking sour-faced. "Well, I never saw a fellow so run after by the girls in this town," she said. Annie sat very still. "You checking up on him?" Aunt Celia looked at Papa.

"Yes. Yes, I am."

"Good." That's all Aunt Celia had to say.

Eva came into the room with her doll. It had a real china face, which Annie had never seen before. She was afraid it would break if she touched it.

The pancakes were soon ready. Annie loved sourdough pancakes as much as Papa did. Napkins fluttered and chairs scraped across the floor as they settled down to eat. Annie couldn't think about anything else but eating for a few minutes while Papa and Aunt Celia talked about the weather, the fruit farm, and Uncle Dan's construction work in town.

Finally Papa said, "Annie, I am going out to do my business. Don't get into any trouble while I'm gone."

Annie stopped. Papa was leaving without her. She wanted to go, but she could tell it would do no good to argue. She would ask Aunt Celia to show her how to knit. That would be all right. But as Papa left, she dug hard into another pancake, and when she tried to swallow, it stuck in her throat.

The day seemed extra long. Aunt Celia was a patient teacher and helped her get a good start on Till's wedding present. Annie had fun with Eva and her toys, but her stomach was homesick.

After lunch Aunt Celia told them to take a nap. The others went to their beds upstairs. But Annie lay down on the front sofa in the parlor and watched the woven curtains throw patterns of shadow and sunlight onto the faded blue carpet. Instead of sleeping, she memorized the shape of every cup sitting behind the glass doors in the cabinet and traced in her mind the paintings on every wall.

The front room was so comfortable and warm that she finally fell asleep on the settee. Voices in the kitchen woke her.

Aunt Celia was saying, "She's been an angel. I thought I'd let her sleep as long as she could. How'd you do today?"

"Well, I got a better price for the mule than I thought I would. This fellow gave me a big bank note. Said he had to leave town in the morning, and this mule was just exactly what he needed. Even if he thought it was a little dog-eared on the corners!" Papa laughed.

"Good, John. Good for you. Did you stop in at Harper's?"

"Yes. I thought nobody was there until I rang the bell at the desk a couple of times. Then Liza Hamblin hurried out from the back room flinging her cape on."

Here Papa paused, and Aunt Celia didn't say anything for a moment either.

"I thought as much," Aunt Celia whispered. "That Liza Hamblin—going to school here, but cutting her classes to spend time at the seed company."

"I'm afraid so," Papa said. "I left, but when I passed by again later, I saw Rye was behind the counter. I just glanced in. I still want to check out the saloon."

Aunt Celia took a second look at Papa. She narrowed her eyes. "Oh, the saloon . . . ?" she began, as though she had hoped Papa would not have to go to the saloon.

Annie didn't move until the conversation was over. When she got up and rubbed the sleep out of her eyes, she caught a glimpse of a stack of books in a nearby cupboard that she had not seen. There was *Paradise Lost*, the big book with the pictures of Adam and Eve. Long ago Papa had taken the dark inky pictures away from her, and closed up the book because he said it wasn't true. Angels didn't really have wings. But still, Annie thought they were the most beautiful drawings she had ever seen. She knew Adam and Eve hadn't drawn pictures of the Garden of Eden. So no one could have known exactly what went on there. But she knew the Devil acted like a snake and fooled them. When they ate the fruit, they had to leave the garden and go into the dreary world. Everything was harder for them after that. Finally the baby Jesus was born to help them get through all the bad things—if they would just listen and do what he asked them to do. The trouble was, you could be obedient, but sometimes you couldn't stop other people like the Devil from sneaking up on you.

Papa's voice came from the kitchen. "Now that

my business is close to done, I'll be able to get back as soon as I cash my note at the bank. The bank was closed before I could make it this afternoon."

"You're welcome to stay as long as you want to stay," Aunt Celia said.

"Well, my supplies won't be ready until day after tomorrow, so it's likely I might stay these two nights."

"Suit yourself, John."

The next two days seemed long for Annie. She liked playing with Eva. And Frank and Culbert didn't bother them. Aunt Celia was patient teaching her to knit. She had the hang of it by the time Papa came home on the second day. But she was glad to know they were going to leave in the morning. Papa had been visiting with some salespeople downtown and she hadn't seen enough of him.

Only one thing made up for all of the homesick hours: the *Paradise Lost* book. Even if it was true that angels didn't have wings, the wings made the pictures feathery and magical, and the wonderful story—that Adam and Eve loved each other enough to stay together even when they went into the ugly world—gave her hope. Mama and Papa were together to help each other in the ugly world. It was a story about mothers and fathers. She hoped it would be the story about Rye and Till, and someday for her, too.

When Papa came in the front door, she was still on the couch on her tummy, looking at *Paradise Lost*. She put it under a pillow when he came into the kitchen. He hung up his coat without a word to anyone—not even Aunt Celia. He wasn't like his usual self. Annie lay against the pillow, pretending she was asleep.

Just before it was time to get ready for dinner,

Annie could hear Aunt Celia talking to Papa. There were some words about Annie's knitting. But Papa didn't say anything. So Aunt Celia kept talking while she set the table. "Dan isn't home yet, but we might as well get on with supper." And finally, "Anything wrong, John?"

For a minute Papa didn't speak. He was keeping something back. After a minute, he hit the table with his fist. "Yes, confound it, and there's not a thing I can do about it!"

"Well, what on earth . . . ?"

"That fellow bought my mule with a bum bank note. And left town. Nobody knows who he is!"

Annie wasn't sure what he meant, but she knew it was trouble. Suddenly she wanted to cry.

"Oh, John!" Aunt Celia stopped stirring the gravy and stared at him. "Oh no, John!"

"I was cleaned out. Taken! No mule, no money." Papa got up from the table and pounded his fist in his hand. "Sometimes . . . sometimes I feel it's too much for God to ask a man to live in this ugly world!" Then he thought about what he had said. "Only I know I asked to be here myself, so I guess I can't complain."

Annie's heart pounded.

The longer Papa argued with himself, the louder and more angry he seemed to be. "I just can't stand here like a lump of clay," he finally said, hitting his fist in his hand. His face looked red as a beet. He rose, then grabbed his coat.

"Supper is about . . ." Aunt Celia began, but stopped.

"Never mind. Never . . .," His voice ended with a sob. He shoved his hands through his coat sleeves and stomped out the front door.

It was a long, sad evening. Annie was homesick

and worried for her father. She was afraid she'd cry if she said anything. She was glad when it was finally time to go to bed, even though Papa wasn't back yet.

After Aunt Celia helped her say her prayers, Annie finally managed to fall asleep in the back porch room, dark and quiet. The Garden of Eden drawings came into her dreams, and the canyon at Aunt Dora's and Uncle Al's. She was dreaming about a long, narrow roadway stretched beside a river with black trees on both sides and rocky cliffs behind the trees. Branches snagged her skirt as she moved down the road. In the dream she tried to cry for help but could make no sound. She was alone. Only the sound of the rushing water flooded up out of the emptiness. She stumbled and fell, then grew tired and wanted to stop walking. But something inside pushed her on. She wanted to wake up. She heard a moan and wondered if it was part of her dream. The skin on her neck was cold, and she was shaking.

Again she heard a low sad moan, then a scratching sound. She knew she was awake now. Someone was trying to come in at the back door!

She wanted to scream, but her fear clogged up her throat. She could see in the moonlight that Papa's bed was still empty. The voice outside the door was louder now—a moaning, hollow sound—familiar in a way. Then she realized why it sounded familiar. It was Papa's voice!

The back door was not locked, she was sure of it. But Papa rattled it as though it were locked. Before she could run to help him, a soft shape brushed against her bed. She didn't move. It hurt to breathe. She heard a quiet question.

"That you, John?"

Aunt Celia. She hurried to open the door. "Shhh.

Don't wake Annie. Oh land, John! What's happened to you!"

"I didn't want to disturb you, Celia."

"John, what's happened?"

Bathed with the moonlight, Papa limped into the back porch room, his shoulders hunched, his hair mussed.

"You're bleeding. You've been in some fight or accident! John, what's happened?"

Papa's breathing was unsteady and choked. "Land, I don't know!"

"What is it, John? You've been to the saloon after Rye Hadley!" Aunt Celia helped Papa walk through the back porch and into the kitchen. He sat on a chair.

"I didn't drink, Celia! Though I wanted to. I'm still tempted. But I didn't drink."

"Did you find Rye?"

"No."

For a moment no one spoke. Annie heard gulping as Papa took some water Aunt Celia gave him from the cup at the pump.

"So what did you do to yourself?"

"I saw . . . the fellow who took my mule."

Silence. Then Annie heard the splash of water and Papa's groans as though Aunt Celia were washing up his wounds.

"It's not a place for a respectable man! No place for a respectable man," Aunt Celia murmured. "Ah, you don't have to tell me who won the fight. You must have lain unconscious a long time." She was quiet for a moment. "I had an inkling you ought not to go there," she admitted. "It's no place for a respectable man. No place." As she worked, she continued to murmur, "John . . . John . . ."

In a few minutes Papa limped from the kitchen into the back porch bedroom again, his head bandaged. He dropped heavily onto the bed, and Aunt Celia took off his boots.

"I'm all right," he breathed.

"Sleep, John. You'll feel better in the morning."

But Papa didn't sleep. When Aunt Celia left, he slipped from the bed onto his knees. "Dear Heavenly Father," he whispered. "Dear Father in Heaven! Please forgive me. I'm a weak man, lashing out like that. My temper . . . I just . . . I don't know. Sometimes things just get to be too much." His head fell in his hands when he said, "Too much," and Annie could not hear any words for a while. She stayed still. He began again. "I came here to judge Rye Hadley. But I'm in no fit condition to judge Rye Hadley or any other man. . . ."

Listening, Annie could hear her own heartbeat. She ached from holding her arms and legs so quiet. For what seemed like hours she did not move, until she realized that her father had gone to sleep while still kneeling at his bedside.

In the morning she heard subdued voices in the kitchen.

"What's good for one headache isn't necessarily good for another."

"Will you please wake Annie? We'd best get started immediately." That was Papa's voice.

When she came to the kitchen doorway, Annie saw Papa at the table with his head in his hands. It was late morning and none of the cousins were in the kitchen. They had all gone out to work or play.

"Good morning, Annie," Aunt Celia said. "Put your clothes on and get your bag together. Your papa will be leaving very soon."

Papa was quiet, and so was she. All through breakfast a sadness hung over them. Only Aunt Celia spoke. "Good-bye, little Annie. See you at harvest time when we come to pick up the supplies. Good-bye."

Annie and her father left, and there were no songs on the way home.

7

At home Papa did not say a word about Rye Hadley. He stayed quiet. Till was quiet, too. The family sang and laughed as they helped Mama make soap, but Till kept her eyes lowered and would not join in.

"Let's all take turns stirring the pot," Mama said. "Who wants to be first?"

Annie did. She liked to be first stirring the dark lye water into the big black pot of tallow on the outdoor fire. Lye water was an ugly brown liquid Mama made up each year by soaking cottonwood ashes in a barrel. It looked like medicine. Mama poured it into the tallow while Annie stirred, and it ran in whirling rivers that sank slowly into the fat and finally disappeared. The lye and tallow were mixed, then cooled on boards and cut up into bars. It was always a miracle to Annie that the ugly lye water and fat could make such good soap when they came together.

"Till, you pour the lye water for Annie while I jack the pot up a bit," Mama said.

"Mama, I . . ." Till's voice stopped in the middle of a sigh.

"Till? What's the matter, honey? It's about Rye, isn't it?"

"It's nothing." Till dropped the spoon into the fat and turned and ran into the house. The door banged shut behind her.

Till was a puzzle to Annie lately. She was so very

irritable. Annie didn't know now if there would be a wedding or not, but in secret she kept knitting on Till's wedding present. It was usually quiet in her hiding place where she could forget Papa's continuing quiet and Till's touchiness.

From the biggest chink in the wall—her special "window"—she watched the autumn world fading. It was the drab season. All of the leaves had already turned colors and fallen down. The north wind blew into the attic, and the rain fell at least once a week.

From another chink in the wall she had a good view of Papa butchering the hogs. Mama did not like the children to watch the hogs being killed. Papa had to hang the hog by its feet from the elm tree, split the long gray hide, and let all of the inside parts fall out onto the grass. Annie had to turn her eyes away.

The quiet dying of autumn hushed everyone in the family. While the dusky evenings grew colder, they sat closer beside the fire. Mama read to them from the Bible or the Book of Mormon, or *Uncle Tom's Cabin*. And they listened to the wind.

Till kept her eyes on her sewing. She didn't speak. Rye didn't come. Papa would not talk about the trip to Fillmore or about Rye—until it came up on the night the family roasted the deer.

Whenever Papa killed a deer, he turned it on a spit over the fire until it was tender and brown and ready to eat. From the fats and juices that dripped into the pan on the hearth, Mama would make gravy to soak their bread. All of them loved this most special feast of the year. They could hardly wait to taste the meat. While it cooked, they listened patiently to Mama while she read *Uncle Tom's Cabin*. As she read tonight, she kept placing and replacing a letter in the book as though she were using it for a bookmark. Till watched her. Even Papa noticed it.

"Why don't you just leave the letter in the book?" Papa asked.

Mama looked up, startled, and stumbled over her reading.

Papa grew curious. "What letter is that, anyway?" He reached over and tried to take it from the book. But Mama wouldn't let him have it. "That . . . it's something I put here to remind me I wanted to talk to you," Mama said. "Later."

"Is that letter from Celia?" He was angry.

Mama drew up in her chair and looked at Papa steadily. "Yes, it's Celia's letter." She paused and then let her words pour out.

"You didn't tell me about this letter when it came, John. I wanted to ask you just what happened when you saw Rye Hadley in Fillmore? Till hasn't heard from him since you came back, and the poor girl has been stricken with wondering and anxiety. I think you know something you're not letting on, because Celia writes here something about . . ." Mama fumbled with the letter to find the spot she wanted to read. *"I hope Till isn't too upset about Rye Hadley and Liza Hamblin."* When she put the letter down, Annie could see anger in her eyes. "John, what on earth have you been keeping from us?"

Annie knew that whatever had upset Mama concerned Till, too. Lately it was hard to tell just what was going on with Till. Annie had often seen her leave the room, suddenly breaking into tears. But right now she just sat very still, listening, looking from Mama's face to the letter in Mama's hands.

Papa tried to control his voice. "I told you I saw Rye Hadley at his work."

"You saw more than that!" Mama was stern. "You must have seen more than that. Celia knows you did, and she was expecting you'd tell us. What did you see? Is Rye Hadley sweet on Liza Hamblin? You let your daughter eat her heart out, pining away for some news, and the news is right on the tip of your tongue, but you don't give it to us."

Papa lowered his voice. "I didn't expect Rye Hadley to stop sending letters to Till." He leaned forward on his knees.

"Well, he hasn't written. He must have seen you spying and figured you'd tell Till that he's sweet on Liza Hamblin, and there's no use going on with anything anymore. There's evidently no more engagement, no more courting, nothing. But how were we supposed to know?"

The room was painfully silent. Mama was so upset, it seemed she could not breathe.

"I don't believe it!" Papa cried. "I never thought in all eternity Rye Hadley would stop coming after Till."

"Well, it's true! He's chasing somebody else, and it would help us if we knew about it," Mama said more quietly. "We're wondering if you said anything to him. We would like to know just what has happened."

"I never said a thing," Papa said. "I saw Rye at Harper's. I told you that. I heard that he frequented the saloon, but I didn't see him there."

Now Mama stiffened. "Did you go near the saloon?"

"I wanted to see if Rye Hadley frequented the saloon," Papa said gruffly. "Rumors have it he's often there in the evenings. He's got his weaknesses. Like every other man I know."

Now Mama leaned back in her chair and opened *Uncle Tom's Cabin*. "We'll discuss it later." Her voice sounded final. "As for Till, I suppose the best thing for you to do is meet somebody else, honey. He wasn't any good, anyway; your pa saw that. Honestly, I don't know what's got into young people anymore nowadays, not able to grow up, get married like normal folks and take responsibility. Why do they have to go through all these games, courting and then not courting?"

At Mama's words about courting, Papa grinned. "Aw, now, Mama, we played a few of those games ourselves, don't you remember?" He laughed. "You yourself kept dilly-dallying around with some lesser fellow, if you'll remember. What was his name? Hart . . . something Hart?"

Mama pretended to ignore him and turned her attention to Till who was fighting back tears. Mama said softly, "You'll get over him honey. Or he'll be coming back, one or the other." Mama paused. "But I would hope you wouldn't want him now. You'll find somebody better."

Till ran toward the stairway. Tearfully, she cried out, "No, I don't want him. I wouldn't have him now if he gave himself to me along with his weight in gold!" She rushed up the stairs.

"Heartaches," Mama sighed. "So many heartaches for a young girl before she marries and settles down."

The meat was almost roasted, but if everyone felt as lumpy inside as Annie did, they weren't thinking about it. At least not while they could still hear Till sobbing in the upstairs bedroom. "Oh, oh, oh," and sometimes, "Oh, Rye. Rye Hadley. Rye."

The next few days were quiet. Laura and Jennifer did much of the work, while Annie watched Farrell.

Mama allowed Till to stay in bed later in the mornings, sometimes until nine o'clock. Annie was sad for Till, but she didn't quite know what to do, except to go ahead and finish Till's blanket as though there would be a Christmas wedding after all. So she did her best to finish the blanket, though in the next three days she didn't get much done. There was always something else. Several times she stayed in her attic corner without answering when someone called, even though it made them angry because they didn't know where she was.

On the day Aunt Celia and Uncle Dan and their family were supposed to come for a visit, Annie decided she didn't have enough of her knitting done to show Aunt Celia. She spent almost all morning working on it in the attic. It was a long, lonely morning of sitting, squinting until her eyes stung. Over and over she missed her stitches, knitting and purling and trying, and sometimes wanting to throw it away. She was startled from her work by a loud clattering on the stairs leading to the bedroom. She hadn't seen anyone come along the road, but somebody must have ridden into the yard, because through her little window in the wall she could see a horse standing by the apple tree.

Up into the bedroom rushed Till, sobbing and trying to shut the door. Something was wrong. Frightened, Annie quickly moved inside the closet and stood with her back flat against the wall to hide herself.

Rye Hadley burst into the room before Till could lock the door. He slammed the door behind him. Till's gasps choked off her breath. "Rye . . . you can't follow me into the bedroom!" Then she looked angry, ready to fight. Annie froze.

"If you'd just give me half a chance to talk to you, you'd know!" His cheeks were flushed. "I love you, Till Wood."

"Rye!" She was wary.

"Yes, I do. And I'm going to marry you!"

Rye Hadley reached out to touch Till, but she backed away. "Till. Till, please. I don't know what rumors your father spread about me. But he never saw me with Liza Hamblin. She was the one to come after me. I tried to stay away from her! It's been hard. Sometimes impossible!" He stopped and closed his eyes. "It's you I love, Till, believe me. What can I do to convince you?" Rye Hadley reached out again to touch Till.

Rye Hadley was big, taller by half a foot than Till. She did not pull away. Gently, he touched her elbows. Her arms moved at his touch, but only a little. She stood scarcely breathing. Her eyes were closed. Finally, her fists relaxed, and her fingers rested on his arm. Rye, slowly, as Annie had seen him do once before, placed his hands over her arms and brought her close. "I love you," he said softly. A shock of light brown hair had fallen over his smooth high forehead. "I love you, and I'm going to marry you. . . ."

Till hadn't yet opened her eyes.

"I'm going to marry you by Christmastime or know why not." He pulled Till closer and closer.

Annie tried to shut her eyes, but she couldn't. Rye folded his arms around Till softly and embraced her. He reached for her mouth. They stood for a long time kissing, and Annie was afraid that one of them would hear her breathing in the closet. They finally pulled apart, and Till rested her head against Rye's shoulder.

"Rye, Rye," she sobbed. Annie could not see her

face now, but she could hear tears in her words. "Oh, Rye, I was so afraid you wouldn't come."

Annie's breathing seemed louder and her heart noisier. What if Till heard her?

"Till, it's not too soon. Let's run away and get married—now. I want you so much." Rye kissed Till's forehead and her ears. He was kissing her face all over.

"Rye, we can't. It's wrong."

"Why not? I love you."

"We should wait until we can be married proper. At Christmastime. You said once . . ."

"I know I said Christmas. But I want you now."

"Not yet. Not yet, Rye. Soon."

"Not yet," Rye said slowly. His arms dropped, and he moved away from Till. "All right," he sighed. "At Christmas. You can have your wedding—a cake, hundreds of people. You'll have everything just as you want. Then," he whispered, "then I'll have you . . . forever."

He kissed her again for a long time. Suddenly they heard footsteps on the stairway.

"What is Papa going to say?" She turned quickly toward the door. "Hide!" Rye dove under the bed while Till frantically dashed for a comb and put her hair into place.

"Till? Why is the door latched?" It was only Jennifer's voice. Annie felt relieved for Till. "Is Rye still here?"

"I came here to get away from him." Till had a good way of telling half the truth.

"Let me in!" Jennifer pounded on the door. "His horse is still in the yard."

"Jenny, leave me alone. I'm upset." Till's voice was shaky. "Please let me alone for a while."

"Let me *in*. I have to get something," Jennifer insisted loudly. Till opened the door. Jennifer looked around, then went to get her shawl out of the dresser drawer. Annie suspected she didn't really need her shawl.

"You'd better find Rye. He was sure looking for you," Jennifer said softly. "I thought I saw him coming into the house while the rest of us were watching Papa unload the hay out in back."

"He did come. I don't feel good," Till said. "Please leave me alone, Jenny."

"Why don't you come downstairs and lie on the sofa? Mama wants to talk to you. She'll be here in a few minutes."

"All right. For a minute," Till said.

Till left with Jennifer as if she didn't know what else to do. Annie was alone in the room with Rye Hadley under the bed. All she could hear was the sound of her heartbeat and his breathing. After a few minutes Rye came out from under the bed, brushing the dust out of his dark blond hair. He fumbled in his vest pocket for a few minutes, then took out a small gold ring.

In a short moment he did a strange thing. He slipped the handkerchief through the ring, tied a knot around the band, and left the handkerchief with the ring tied in it on Till's pillow. Then he opened the window and climbed outside. It was a long way to the ground. Somehow he must have jumped or slid down the corner of the house, because in a few moments he was gone, and when Annie looked through the chink again, neither Rye Hadley nor his horse were anywhere to be seen.

8

*E*lizabeth Ann Wood Preston took a long breath. *Clara was leaning over her, tucking the coverlets around her feet. None of the personages now seemed to be anywhere about. It was quiet as it had been quiet then, except that she could hear a radio somewhere in the background playing "Silent Night, Holy Night."*

How silent, how far away the stars, Elizabeth Ann thought. She had never felt such silence as she had felt after Rye's visit.

After Rye Hadley left, Annie crept out of the closet into the room and over to the window. Though she could not see Papa unloading the hay, she knew he was doing it so that Aunt Celia's boys could sleep on the haystack. Everybody was standing around the hay wagon now, watching or helping. Even Mama helped sometimes, but not often, mostly standing by with Farrell for encouragement.

Annie's eyes would not stop looking toward Rye's handkerchief, and her feet would not obey. She wanted to touch Rye's ring and the handkerchief, which was bright blue covered with red and white flowers. Steadily, her hands lifted the blue handkerchief from Till's pillow so that she could see the ring. It was beautiful. On a narrow band of gold lay a tiny diamond in the center of a setting of carved blossoms.

The only diamond they had ever seen in the family before had been Aunt Celia's wedding band with one small stone. But that ring was not as pretty as this one.

The special voice of the angel of heaven inside of her—the Holy Ghost—told Annie to put down the handkerchief and leave the room. But her eyes and hands would not obey. She slipped the ring out of the knot and onto her thumb. It was too big, even for her thumb, but it made her imagine being grown up, being in love, being married.

Just then she heard footsteps on the stairs and in the doorway. It was too late to hide or to run, so she turned around quickly. It was Till.

"Annie!" Till's eyes widened. "What . . . what are you doing?"

Annie wanted to run away and cry, but she didn't know where she would go.

"Where have you been, Annie Wood? How long have you been here? Did you see anyone?"

These were a lot of questions. Maybe Till thought Mr. Hadley was still under the bed. No, his horse was gone. More than likely she wanted to know if Annie saw Rye Hadley leave, or if Annie had seen him at all.

"Did you just now come up?"

"Yes," Annie lied. She didn't know why she couldn't think of clever things to say that did not make her a liar.

Till's eyes flashed. "Did you see anybody?"

"No," Annie lied again.

"What's that you're holding behind your back, Annie Wood?"

It was the handkerchief—all wadded up in her hand, wrinkled from her sweat.

"I found this on your pillow," she whispered, opening her hand.

Till's eyes softened. "Annie! It's . . . oh, never mind! Just give it to me!" She took the handkerchief and smoothed the wrinkles out of it. "It's something of mine. Now leave me alone for a minute."

"I . . ." Annie had not really told Till all she ought to tell her, but Till waved her out of the room with her hands.

"Please, Annie!" Her voice was hard and sounded tired. "Just leave me alone."

The ring was still on Annie's thumb! The doorway seemed to whirl before her eyes. Her feet wanted to go, but her body wouldn't follow.

"Annie!" Till's voice was low and harsh this time. "Annie, go!"

Annie decided she had no choice but to leave, and so she did. Her feet carried her out into the stairwell and down the stairs as rapidly as they could go without stumbling. The rooms downstairs seemed too bright. When she slipped the ring into her pocket, she felt cold and afraid. She was afraid to go into the kitchen where Mama was working, but there wasn't any other place, and she wanted to be near someone. Tonight was the special night Aunt Celia Olson and the cousins were coming, so Mama was awfully busy.

"Where in heaven's name have you been, Annie Wood?" Mama asked.

"I went upstairs for a minute." Her throat was dry, but Mama didn't notice. She asked her to set the table.

The silverware felt heavy as Annie carried it from place to place. As she put down the napkins, she heard a loud commotion in the front yard. Now Aunt Celia and Uncle Dan and Culbert and Frank and Emmett were here, and Bertha would be toddling along behind Eva. So Annie stopped setting the table and went to the door with everyone else, including

Till, who came down looking sleepy-eyed.

With all the hearty greetings, Annie lost her feeling of despair. John and Peter took Culbert and Frank and Emmett into the back to finish stacking up the hay where all six of them would sleep tonight while Aunt Celia and Uncle Dan and the two girls would use the boys' bedroom.

At supper, the boys asked Mama the same question they always asked: "Auntie, may we have bread and milk for supper?" They thought it was a treat. They didn't know the Woods had it every day. Mama was amused. She already had some bread and milk ready for them.

After supper they asked if they could play "Run Sheep Run" in the front yard. Mama and Aunt Celia said yes, if they would promise to come in when it got dark. Everyone tramped outside, running and tumbling. They screamed and laughed until their sides ached—until the mothers stopped them and made them come to bed. Annie forgot every bad thing that happened today when she was running and rolling in the front yard with everyone else. The boys teased Eva and Annie because they could never get the best of anybody—they were both so short.

When Mama stepped out on the front doorstep and hit the spoon on her black skillet, Annie was suddenly aware of the red sun setting in the west and the cool autumn darkness that closed over the yard where the leaves from the currant bushes lay scattered and broken.

Out of breath, the whole troop clattered over the doorstep. The boys took some bedding Mama had piled up near the doorway and ran with it in their arms out to the haystack, laughing.

It took everyone a long time to settle down.

When she climbed the stairs with Eva and took her nightgown out of the closet, Annie could still hear the boys on the haystack laughing and talking, and Laura and Jennifer and Till still talking downstairs with the grownups. Annie begged Mama to let Eva sleep in her bed with her, and she hoped it wouldn't be too crowded. Even though Eva was older than she was and somewhat taller, she was not very big.

After Eva unbuttoned Annie's buttons and helped her slip out of her dress, Annie suddenly remembered Till's ring in her pocket. She put her hand in her pocket to take it out. But it wasn't there. For a while she would not admit to herself that it wasn't there. She felt with both hands in both pockets, and said to herself that the ring must be hiding.

But her heart skidded to a stop. She could not stop feeling her empty pockets.

"What are you looking for?" Eva finally asked her.

"I lost something." She didn't need to lie to Eva.

"What was it?"

"Something I lost." She didn't need to tell all of the truth, either.

"It must have come out of your pocket while you were running," Eva said.

Annie was still breathless and afraid. What was going to become of her when Mr. Hadley found out?

"I have to go look for it," she whispered. Her voice sounded far away and hoarse.

"You'd better wait for tomorrow. It's too dark."

"I really ought to find it."

"What was it?"

Eva wanted to know everything. But Annie couldn't tell her.

"I guess I'd better wait until morning," she tried to say through the lump in her throat. She climbed into her nightgown and knelt by her bed to say her prayers. It crossed her mind to ask Heavenly Father to help her find that ring. But how could she ask Heavenly Father's help to find something she had taken that wasn't hers?

Although the sheets were warmer with Eva in the bed, there wasn't much room, so she lay straight on the edge until she could hear Eva's breathing close to the wall, soft and long. She was still awake when Jennifer and Laura came into the room. Finally Till came.

"Till, what was it Aunt Celia was telling Mama about Liza Hamblin?" Jennifer was asking. "It sounded like it was something about a baby."

"Hush. It's nothing," Till said in a harsh whisper.

"I didn't hear anything," Laura put in.

"It's none of our business," Till said quietly. Then she said something else that Annie couldn't hear very well. It sounded like ". . . rumor. . . ."

When all three girls were in the big bed and Annie was no longer able to hear their whispers, she wanted to fall asleep, but could not seem to close her eyes. She waited and waited for sleep, but it didn't come.

In the moonlight, Annie could clearly see her shoes, as though they were waiting to be slipped on. Soon, giving in to some overwhelming mystery she could not understand, she knew she was on her way outside to look for the ring. If somebody heard her, she could tell them she was on her way to the privy. Without stopping to think about it any more, she climbed out of bed and slipped on her sweater.

It seemed like a hundred miles from the top of the stairway to the door stoop. She held her breath every step of the way. Then she opened the door slowly so it would not squeak.

There was such a large moon that it was not that dark outside. When she got down on her hands and knees, she could see the pebbles in the grass. It would be like hunting for a needle in a haystack. She remembered she hadn't gone near the haystack tonight. She had been running in the yard. And once Eva had chased her down close to the river.

As she looked down toward the river, she saw something shining in the moonlight. Her heart skipped a beat, and she ran toward it. But it was not the ring. It was an empty snake skin. For a moment she was afraid. But it was ugly and beautiful at the same time, and she couldn't stop staring. That dead hull looked so much like a live snake—or a hundred shimmering rings mocking her from the shadows.

For a few minutes she ran her fingers through the crabgrass and weeds and dry leaves. Her eyes began to sting from looking so hard. Then she sat back on her heels and let the tears come. There was no one anywhere awake who knew she was crying. She felt lonely and old, more than ninety years old, as though she were just getting started on a long journey that would last through an eternity of seasons.

. Down toward the valley she could hear the river licking the stones and slipping past the lilac bushes where the leaves had turned brown and gold and fallen like brittle paper. It would soon be winter. That night she would like to have stopped the world from moving. She would like to go to the river, sit and watch the water, be herself beside it forever without any changing. She wouldn't care right then if she didn't do all the things in the world she had planned to do—all the things people grow into doing. It seemed that everything had something wrong with it—some flaw in it.

Somewhere one of the cows mooed a long, sad cow-sound.

In a minute she thought she might answer the cow with a girl sound full of the same sadness.

But she felt a heaviness like sleep in her eyes, so she carefully walked back into the house and lay down beside Eva. The next thing she knew, it was morning.

9

All morning Annie was in a hurry to look for Till's ring. But Mama didn't let her get away without drying dishes, so she dried them and put them away in the cupboard. As she worked, she could hear Mama's worried voice telling Aunt Celia, "It's unbelievable! Just unbelievable!"

"Well," Aunt Celia replied, "Mrs. Hadley is not going to let Liza Hamblin railroad Rye into anything until they can see that Liza is telling the truth."

"You wouldn't think a girl would want that kind of truth to be mouthed around."

"She's a peppery one, that Liza Hamblin. She stops at nothing. Rye denies the whole thing. He says if there is any truth in what she says about her condition," Aunt Celia assured her, "it belongs to somebody else."

"Tsk. It's just unbelievable."

Annie wasn't sure Mama needed her for anything else, but she could see Mama was so busy talking with Aunt Celia that she wouldn't miss somebody as small as Annie. So Annie slipped out the back door and into the front yard. She kept her eyes on the ground and shuffled the dust with her feet, walking over every single spot in the yard.

In a few minutes Eva came around from the back, dragging her baby sister Bertha.

"Did you find it yet, Annie?"

"No," she answered.

Bertha was clinging to Eva's fingers with one hand. Her other fingers were in her mouth.

"A little round golden ring," she said, quickly so she could get the words out.

"A little round ring," Eva said quite calmly.

It seemed to be a long morning. Step by step Annie looked over every inch of ground. She repeated prayers to herself silently without opening her mouth.

Then, interrupting her concentration, she heard Eva yell, "Berty, Berty," And when Annie looked up, she saw little Bertha running toward the river, her sashes and petticoats flying.

"Berty! You come back here! You are too little to play in the crick. Not for you. Bad. Bad. Come to Eva!"

Eva rubbed the mud from one of Bertha's shoes. Then she stopped and lifted something that had fallen from the shoe. "Is this what you were looking for, Annie?"

It was the ring, all right. Annie was stunned. Inside of her was a flood of feeling that felt ready to be unleashed. She wanted to cry, to shout, but for now she kept it in.

"That's it!" Annie breathed, not sure how she should feel that Eva found it instead of her.

Eva was impressed. "Where did you get it?" Eva's voice made the question sound guarded. "It looks like something that belongs to my mama. In fact, I am sure this is my mama's ring. Where did you find it?"

"I can't remember." Annie lied again.

"Well, I'd better give it back to my mama."

"All right."

It seemed Annie could say "all right" without any trouble. It came out on the tip of her tongue without any worry about what was going to happen when Till found out from Rye Hadley that somewhere there was a ring, and she didn't have it, and Annie didn't have it, and nobody here had it. She simply said "All right," and felt a daylight feeling full of fresh air in her mind. She could hear Eva in the background saying, "It's so pretty. It looks like that ring that belongs to Mama. I'm sure that's Mama's. I'll see if it's missing from her jewel case at home first, and then she'll never know it was missing."

Annie felt that as soon as Aunt Celia Olson and Uncle Dan took everyone back to Fillmore this afternoon, she would be free. She wanted to forget everything she had ever had to do with the ring—with watching Till, and with knowing all the hundreds of things Annie knew that made a heavy darkness in her heart. When she imagined she was free, she grew sleepy.

Annie followed Eva into the house. When Eva decided it was her mama's ring, she wanted to keep it. But Annie didn't care. She didn't care at all. While nobody was looking, she went quietly up the stairs and into her attic closet with a blanket, rolled up on the floor, and was asleep in a minute.

The next thing she heard was a lot of shouting and laughing.

"We found her! We found her! Get up, Annie Wood, and come say good-bye."

Annie opened her eyes slowly, and suddenly a row of legs and arms emerged into visible cousins and brothers, one after another, pointing, rocking her chair, and examining her hiding spot. At the door she could see Eva's silhouette.

"Hey, I didn't know this was here," Emmett Olson was standing at the chinks and knothole windows. "Wowee! You can see clear to Coyote."

"Is this where you hide to do your knitting, Annie Wood?"

"What a super cave. Let's play pirates."

"Annie, Mama wants you to come," Laura said. "Aunt Celia's leaving, and she wants to say good-bye."

So much noise. The big boys turned, stirring up dust with their shoes. Then they went into the bedroom and down the stairs, laughing and shouting. Peter and Farrell followed.

Eva waited for her. "Come and say good-bye to Mama." There was never a minute to show Aunt Celia her knitting.

It seemed to take a long time for Uncle Dan's family to leave. Out in the crisp fall air Annie's eyes came open, and she could see everyone clambering into the wagon, hollering and shouting. Mama couldn't seem to let go of talking with Aunt Celia. She said, "Yes, well, it's been lovely to have you. I'm sorry Dan has to be back so soon."

"I'll get those scissors to you when I come down for the wedding," Aunt Celia replied.

Mama sounded strange. "There sure won't be a wedding if that rumor proves out to be true."

"Well, if there's a wedding, we'll all be here. You can count on us," Aunt Celia promised.

"Ought to get together at Christmastime, wedding or not."

It seemed that Mama and Aunt Celia would never stop talking. The boys in the wagon were getting restless. Finally Uncle Dan called, "Hop in, Mother." He came around to take her elbow.

Mama gave Aunt Celia a hug.

"Thanks again for the meat and cheese."

"I'm going to enjoy those apples!" Mama said.

Then as an afterthought she added, "Since we didn't get a start with our apples this year, thanks to Bugaboo." She had her hand on Annie's hair.

Annie tried to grin, even though she was thinking about all of the other bad things that she had done. If Mama knew about her most recent terrible deed, she wouldn't joke. Annie waved at Eva. There was a lot of bouncing in the wagon while Uncle Dan got into the driver's seat and pulled away calling to the mules, hitting them across the neck with the reins.

Till and Jennifer and Laura were out of the house now, standing in the background together and waving.

"See you at Christmastime next, then, wedding or not."

Till didn't answer. It had upset her that a terrible rumor had spoiled the air. Without smiling, she lifted her hand. "Good-bye."

10

*E*lizabeth Ann turned her head. Her mouth felt dry. There was water on the table, but she couldn't reach it. Suddenly, someone was there holding the glass to her lips, the glass cool, the water soothing on her tongue. She closed her eyes as she swallowed.

When Annie awoke and opened her eyes on the first Sunday in December, Jennifer and Till and Laura were gone, their bed made. From downstairs Annie heard Mama banging in the kitchen, and Papa stamping his feet inside the door on his way from the woodpile. She lifted her head. It was snowing! Big furry flakes crowded the gray sky. Their first snow. She could almost taste the cold wet ice of winter on her tongue.

For a while she snuggled down further into her flannel sheets, covering her mouth and eyes and hands. She thought how warm she was and how cold she would be when she hurried downstairs, her teeth chattering. She kept her breath shallow so that she wouldn't suck in too much cold air. But she soon wanted to be downstairs with the others, so she jumped out of bed fast, dragged on socks and shoes and flew down the stairs until she was sitting in front of the fire with everyone else.

As she listened to the voices around her, she felt

comfortable. Mama was telling Papa and John to be on time to priesthood. Today was fast and testimony meeting. No breakfast.

"Oh, Mama." Laura didn't like to fast at all. "Please don't make us starve."

"I'm not making anybody starve. It's the Lord's will we should learn to go without, and I'm not one to keep the teachings of the Lord from my own family. You can learn to give a little. It won't hurt you. Remember, the Savior fasted forty days and forty nights, and he hasn't asked you to fast that long."

"It wasn't really forty days!" John declared.

"Nobody told me it wasn't forty days," Mama reprimanded. "I take what the Bible says to be the truth. It won't hurt you to go without your breakfast. Get dressed, and you'll forget your stomachs."

Laura and Jennifer started upstairs after their Sunday dresses and woolen underwear. Till was helping Mama feed Farrell. Lately Till had been keeping away from everybody else and staying quiet. Annie knew she was terribly worried about Rye. No one had seen or heard from him since he had kissed her in the bedroom. Because of the ring, Annie was glad he hadn't come, but she did feel sad when Papa came back with the mail every other day and there was nothing for Till. Till had told everybody she wouldn't write to Rye Hadley until he wrote to her. But he didn't write.

"Now, Papa," Mama encouraged. "You and John better hurry if you're going to make priesthood. We'll be ready when you come back for us at ten."

Papa looked starched and clean, his shaven face set above his scrubbed neck, already red from rubbing against his shirt collar. John looked as clean as Papa, and even more uncomfortable.

"I'll see you in a bit over an hour. Not a one of

you be late getting on your duds." Papa stomped out to the wagon, hitched and ready to travel the half mile into Coyote to the old adobe church house.

Annie was hungrier than a bear in spring, but she didn't dare say so. She tried to forget it all the time she was running upstairs to get her clothes, running downstairs to put them on, and warming her feet and hands by the fire. It was hard for her to forget her empty stomach when she was on her way out the door. It was hard to forget when she had to sit still in the long, long meeting while the people in Coyote bore their testimonies. All she wanted was for everything to end so she could go home and eat something, because her stomach felt hollow as an empty bucket. But the meeting didn't end; it didn't end, and it did not end.

Papa sometimes stood and bore his testimony. He did it this morning. "Brothers and sisters. I feel I must stand today and thank my Father in Heaven for all the blessings he gives me. I'm so grateful for my family. I pray all of us will choose the right. Of course, it's hard to live perfect. We live our lives imperfect because we haven't done it before."

Papa paused a long time. "But Jesus showed us the way to be perfect. And I'm going to keep trying. You can't sit down and give up. There's lots of work to do . . . with ourselves and each other forever. Everybody must take his load. I'm thankful Jesus Christ died for my mistakes."

Here Papa got a catch in his voice as though he might not go on. "I know as sure as I stand here this gospel is true, because when I live it, the blessings come like the Lord promised. And when I don't live it, they don't."

Mama's hand rested on Annie's knee. She gave

the knee a light squeeze. When Papa's testimony ended, it seemed as though everybody on the bench began breathing more easily.

But there was still more meeting, more meeting, and more meeting, until Annie wanted to cry. But she knew it was important to Heavenly Father that everyone was heard. She leaned against the bench while some nice older lady talked and talked, telling everyone about the lonely years her husband was gone on a mission while she had to stay home and tend the little children. But it was worth it—there were so many blessings. The mare had twins and she sold them both just in time to keep the family from starving. *Oh, starving.* When the lady finished her talking, there was a loud bang at the back of the church by the door, and a gust of cold air. Annie turned around.

Everybody turned. The lady said, "In the name of Jesus Christ, amen."

Someone had just stepped inside the chapel doors. He was covered with snow. He brushed off his coat, took off his hat, and hit it against his hand. Then he ran thick fingers through his wet hair. Some people watched him for only a moment. Some people stared at him longer. Annie couldn't take her eyes off of him.

"My dear brothers and sisters," a rusty voice from the front of the chapel interrupted the silence. It was Brother Clawson, one of the old men who lived in Kingston. Everyone turned to listen to him while he bore his testimony. Even Annie turned to look at him, and when she did, she could see Till. Till was clutching her handkerchief so tightly that it would not have surprised Annie if she could wring water out of it. Mama reached across Laura and gently touched Till on the knee. In Mama's face there was a hard, angry tightness around her mouth.

Even with Mama's comfort, Till looked so pale Annie was frightened. Laura turned around, her face full of wondering. "It's him all right," Laura whispered, almost out loud.

Mama whispered, "Shhh."

Annie turned around again. The man who came so late into the meeting was still standing quietly at the door. His face was red with cold and seemed darker because of his angry look. Now Annie could see who it was. It was Rye Hadley. Her heart thumped. Now everyone would know about the ring.

"The Lord has been good to me and my family," Brother Clawson went on. At the other end of the bench, John leaned forward as though he wanted to ask Papa questions. Peter watched Till and giggled, but Papa quieted them. Jennifer kept her hand on Till's wrist.

It was like an eternity before old Brother Clawson stopped talking, and then Annie was afraid someone else would stand up. She wanted the meeting to end, but when it did, Rye Hadley would ask Till, "Where is the ring I gave you?" Just thinking about it prickled the hair on the back of Annie's neck and raised goose bumps on her arms.

Finally Bishop Culbert Lane stood up, and the meeting ended with song and prayer. Annie didn't move for a moment while everyone got up around her and pushed and shoved to leave the benches and get into the aisles. Then she turned and looked over her bench toward the back of the chapel.

She could see Rye Hadley shoulder his way against the current of people who were leaving, working his way through the crowd, his light brown hair still glistening with melted snow.

Mama was waiting for Annie to get up and go so

that she and Laura and Till could get out into the crowded aisle. Annie got up and made her way through the stiff dresses and long dark coats just in time to see Rye edge into the empty bench behind them. He reached out and took Till by the hand. His eyes were still full of anger, but when he saw Till, he softened, and his voice grew quiet.

"Hello, Brother and Sister Wood," he said to Mama and Papa.

"Well, hello Rye," Mama acknowledged, though her voice sounded tense. "We haven't seen you for a long time." She measured each word, trying to talk past the tightness around her mouth.

"Well, if it isn't Rye Hadley," Papa said curtly.

"I've been busy," he answered quickly. "But you'll see a lot of me now."

"Oh?" Mama tried to be polite, but didn't smile. Papa looked suspicious.

"I quit my job in Fillmore and moved back with my mother in Circleville." Rye's news gave Till a start, and she lowered her eyes. "If you don't mind, I need to talk with Till today."

"Well, I suppose I don't mind. She's certainly been wondering when you'd come," Mama smiled stiffly. "We're going to have supper in a couple of hours when we get home." She paused. "If you'd like to have supper . . . ?"

Papa's brows knit with disapproval when he heard Mama's invitation. But there was a grateful look in Till's eyes.

"Why, thank you, ma'am. I'd be grateful. May I have permission to bring Till with me in my own rig?" Mama began to object, but Rye interrupted her. When he turned to Till, it seemed he was ready to unleash a flood of emotion. "I would have come sooner today except I saw your Aunt Celia Olson this morning."

Till's eyes widened.

"I have to talk to you. Do you mind coming with me in my uncle's two-seater? Say yes."

Till blushed and nodded.

Annie saw a brightness pass between Rye and Till. It was nothing anyone could ever have put a finger on. Nothing solid, but something just as real as solid. Mama stopped to talk with somebody before they left the meetinghouse, and she saw Rye take Till ahead, directing her by her elbow and leaning over her so that his lips touched the hair over her ear.

While Mama and Annie and the others stood in the chapel doorway, Annie could see Rye lift Till into the two-seat buggy. Then he took her hand in his and rubbed it warm before he walked around to the other side and climbed in with her. Annie felt nervous when she watched them drive away.

Now it seemed there wasn't a long enough time until dinner. Annie didn't want to go home and find Till upset at her, and so she was relieved when the two hadn't yet arrived. Then she was afraid to see dinnertime come, praying Till and Rye would not know how she had played a part in what had happened. But she was sure they would know, and it hurt her to think about it.

It was all too soon that she heard the buggy wheel into the yard, and Laura, standing by the window, called out, "Mama, they're here!"

Everybody else was glad, because it meant they could eat, so there was a rush of going and coming—coming through the door, pushing out chairs, pushing in chairs—hellos and how-do-you-dos. Till looked as bright as an apple in winter, blushing and beautiful, locks of dark hair framing her pale face, and rosy high spots braising her cheeks.

Annie tried to look in Till's eyes to see what she might be thinking, but the older sister was too excited to glance at the younger sister.

"Look, Mama!" Till exclaimed, happily giving Mama her hand. On the fourth finger was that ring!

"Oh, Till!" Mama tried to cover her surprise. "Till, my, how lovely. So soon after . . ." But Till didn't stop to listen.

"Look, Papa! I'm engaged. Truly. It's a real diamond!"

"Whoa, now, Till. Whoa, now!"

Papa was completely ignored. All that anybody wanted to do was to see Till's ring. She presented it with a flourish. Jennifer and Laura were clapping with squeals of delight.

"It's real!"

"It's pretty!"

When Till showed the ring to Annie, she said, "Annie Wood, one of these days I'm going to have a talk with you!"

Rye, who was standing close by, leaned over her. "You rascal!" he said to her and tugged one of her curls lightly. Annie began to shake. But in a kind of miraculous way, Rye didn't seem to be angry. "If it hadn't been for Aunt Celia taking it to Mr. Riley to assess its value. . . ! Lucky for us he remembered who he sold it to!" Rye paused just a little to let the next words sink in. "You could have stopped us cold, Annie Wood." She still couldn't tell how angry he really was. "Why don't you mind your own business, you rascal kids? Just let us alone."

"Come to dinner, children."

Rye took Till's elbow. Her happiness seemed to over-ride the disappointments of the past. She turned without saying another thing and walked to the table where Rye pulled out the chair for her to sit.

Till might feel all right now, but Annie felt run over with the hay wagon. She hadn't eaten breakfast, but she had a lump inside that made it hard to eat anything. She could barely hear all the talking. But she heard the silences. Especially Mama's strained silence. Even stronger than her own worry and trembling about what she had done to hurt Till, there was a strained caution in Mama. The air was so heavy that it hurt. Papa did most of the talking.

"So you quit your job in Fillmore and came to Circleville to live with your mother? So how do you plan to keep a family of your own?"

Rye said his uncle in Idaho had a farm, and he needed some young man to run it for him. "I plan to run that farm and begin running it in February or March when the weather breaks. And I want to take Till with me."

Papa frowned. "You ought to wait and see how the farm goes before you take on any extra responsibility. Times are hard now. I don't like this. I don't like it at all. Yes, I gave my permission once, but it was because I couldn't see how I was going to stop it. But I don't like it."

All the time Papa talked, Mama was quiet for the most part, not raising her eyes. Finally she said, very softly, "Why don't you tell him the real trouble, John . . ."

"Tell him?" For a moment Papa didn't seem to understand.

Mama sighed. "Well, I'll tell him. Rye . . ." She tried to get her voice under control. "Rye, we can't accept you graciously into the family. We don't want you to marry our daughter. Oh, it's fine, the ring, the fun of courting. But it can't come to anything." Here it got harder for Mama. She sat up straighter. "There have been certain rumors. . . ."

"Mama, this is no place to bring it up!" Papa interrupted. "The children . . ."

"Nobody needs to know the details," Mama snapped at Papa. "But I've been waiting too long. You know what I mean, Rye Hadley. You know. . . ."

Rye looked dumbfounded.

Mama almost stood up out of her chair. "I'm talking about Liza Hamblin!"

Now Rye did a strange thing. He let his head fall into his hands. His fingers covered his face.

Annie waited to hear Papa say, "Get your elbows off the table, young man." But nobody said anything. It was just quiet, and they heard a little hard wheeze in Rye's breath behind his hands. Then he made a sound like a groan.

Till was staring, her eyes fixed on Rye. When he took his hands from his face, his words were strained. "Mrs. Olson must have told you when she was down here from Circleville."

"It doesn't matter who told me," Mama said.

It was still quiet while everyone watched. Nobody said anything. Rye sighed again. "I know what Liza was saying. She told me. How can I convince you it isn't true? It isn't true. I swear to you it isn't true." There was a choke in his voice.

Suddenly Annie wanted to cry for Rye. She didn't know what he'd been through in Fillmore, but it seemed like a lot. A split second later Till stood up.

"We've had enough now." For all the bright daggers in her eyes, and the tightness in her hands, Till's voice seemed soft. "I've had enough from all of you now." She looked straight at Annie. Annie shrank back into her chair. "Every time Rye and I turn around we meet some obstacle," she said between her teeth. Then she looked at Mama and Papa. "We've had enough from you, Mama, Papa, and I'm going to tell you now . . ." For a minute Annie saw Till as a grown-up lady full of the same fire Mama sometimes had. "I want all of you to listen and not to forget what I say. I'm going to marry Rye Hadley at Christmas. If you won't have the wedding, we'll go to the bishop anyway by ourselves. Later we want to go to the temple when it's finished. We are going to live in Circleville in a little house on his mother's land until we go to the Idaho farm in the spring. It's all settled. It's what I want. It's what's going to happen, and no matter what you do now . . ." Annie thought Till was probably looking right at her, but she was afraid to raise her eyes, ". . . nothing will change it."

Out of the corner of her eye, Annie saw Rye take Till's hand.

11

Grandma, hello. Elizabeth Ann heard the voice, but could not seem to open her eyes. "Grandma, I brought some lunch for you." It was Clara's oldest girl. She had brought her baby with her. When she stepped into the room with the baby in one arm and hot bread in the other, Elizabeth Ann thought she could see more people crowding behind them. Many people. Her friends from Boise, from Albion, from Antimony. She thought she recognized some of them vaguely. Behind them were others, the ones in the white robes. But she didn't know any of them. There was the stranger, the young man she didn't know. Suddenly the young man looked like her Papa as he used to be, and she was fading into the memories of the past again. This time she remembered sitting by Papa on the wagon seat that Christmastime.

The air broke like a cold wet river over Annie's face and pushed back her hair until she felt smooth as a stone, tasting the ice on her tongue. In the background she caught a whiff of the bread Mama had put into the baskets for Mr. Barlow and his family who lived in Kingston. There were also a couple of loaves for another poor family Annie did not know.

Papa was still and tall and dark sitting beside her. She had never been on a Christmas journey with Papa all by herself. She listened to the quiet over everything, trying to memorize what it sounded like: the *shush shush shush* of the hooves and the *crunch, clatch, crunch, clatch* of wheels in packed snow. She thought she would always remember the stillness—the moon glittering white over the fence posts rising across the countryside like broken teeth in a giant comb.

They had not been gone long when Papa said to her, "You're awful quiet, Elizabeth Ann."

It startled her to hear him say her grown-up name.

"What are you thinking about?"

"Oh, nothing."

"That's awful quiet for nothing," Papa said.

As a matter of fact, she was thinking about Rye and Till and what was going to happen to them. There was a blank wondering somewhere deep inside of her that gnawed and gnawed at her until she could not keep away all of the memories that crowded her. Yesterday afternoon, Mama had been sewing up Till's wedding clothes—the lacy ones for underneath—and John's friend, Burton, said behind his hand so Mama couldn't hear, "Them little things? Rye Hadley'll tear them off her in a hurry." John howled with laughter.

The crude comment made Annie remember Rye's hands so tight on Till's waist, his mouth so hungry. She didn't know what would happen when Till was married. And not knowing was frightening. But knowing might be more frightening.

Papa looked down at her, so she finally said, "What do people do when they get married?"

The blackness of her thoughts kept her from exploring all of them, even to herself. When she finished those words, she prayed in the deepest spot in her heart that perhaps Papa wouldn't tell her, but if he did tell her, that it would be lovely and all right.

"He will marry her. There is a wedding. The bishop comes to the house. It's a sacred ceremony."

That wasn't it. "It is special," Mama had said. "It is sacred." But that didn't seem to be the complete answer.

"What does it mean to marry somebody?"

Papa's voice seemed far away. Only his hands were close to her. So she watched the movement of his strong fingers pulling and loosening the reins with perfect control while the horse turned or slowed or started again in rhythm with Papa's hands. When she looked up, she could see Papa's beard bobbing below his heavy mouth when he talked. It rose and fell, rose and fell.

"When a young man and a young girl want to live together and have babies, like your mama and I had Till and you and all the others, they must first make promises to stand by each other—so they won't just leave each other when it gets a little difficult raising all those babies. So they make promises to each other at a wedding." Papa paused. "They go together and live in a little house all by themselves, just the two of them, until their children come to live with them."

Annie knew children came from under mothers' aprons, for she had seen Farrell grow inside of Mama. She did not know how he got there, but she didn't ask.

Papa continued. "Someday a young man who is worthy to marry you will come to you and say, 'Miss Elizabeth Ann Wood, will you be my betrothed bride?'" The way Papa said that made her laugh. "'Miss Elizabeth Ann Wood, I love you desperately, madly!'" She was giggling. "'I want to whisk you away into my own kingdom. I want to love you now and

The Light in the Room 109

forever—forever for eternity, Miss Elizabeth Ann Wood.'"

Papa's eyes were twinkling that old happy twinkle she loved so much. "Then you will curtsy nicely." Papa stopped and looked at her sideways. "Can you curtsy, Annie?" When she nodded her head, he commenced his grand talk. "You will curtsy and say, 'Of course,' and then he will make promises to you at the wedding. Important promises. And then someday when he can travel to Salt Lake City, you will probably see the temple all finished. Then you and he and the children will be sealed together for time and eternity in the temple just like Mama and I were sealed in the endowment house many years ago."

Maybe it was the talk about the endowment house, or the temple. *Sealed.* There was something about being *sealed* that no one would tell. Although of course it must be wonderful. She had understood from learning about Aunt Dora and Uncle Al's family that it meant everyone would be together again. But she was not sure what they did to be *sealed*. She tried to block out of her mind all of the troubling questions that did not seem to bode well for Till's happiness. She tried to forget Burton's comment that Rye would tear off her pretty things. She tried to believe Mr. Hadley would not hurt Till nor her wedding clothes.

"Be patient, all right? Be patient for learning what it is to be married and sealed." For a moment Papa leaned close to her, and for an instant she caught the image of his dark face those many months ago when he scolded her for cutting the apple blossoms out of the tree. That memory subdued her.

"Any more questions, Annie?" There were, but she did not want to ask any more. She repeated *Silent Night* to herself and hummed it aloud after a time so that she could replace that empty space where there were still questions. Soon everything seemed to be all right because Papa began to hum with her.

Beneath the moonlight, the mill town of Kingston looked like a jewel case carved out of ice. The roofs of the houses glistened with heavy snow, and the lights in the windows glowed and sparkled like broken glass scattered in the darkness. Papa turned the wagon around several corners, almost as though he went in circles with no plan as to where they were going. But he must have known, because soon, when the edges of the fields stretched into the dark hills, he stopped.

A little cabin sat back among a few trees. When he lifted Annie out of the wagon, she felt suddenly safe and happy with him and wanted to wrap her arms around his neck and kiss him. She didn't. But when she thought about him being her papa, it warmed her heart. He was the best papa. She felt sorry she had often been afraid of him. But always, while she was afraid of him, at the same time she loved him.

"Let's see. Can we get the carrot pudding and the oat cake?" Papa asked, moving baskets and breads around in the box at the foot of the wagon seat. She walked to the doorway with her hand curled in his.

"Brother Joe?" Papa's big fist pounded the door only once, and Brother Joe Barlow appeared in the sliver of light that cast a halo on the snowy trees. His leathery face seemed pinched around his narrow eyes of steel gray.

"Well, well, if it isn't John Wood and his Annie! Come in!" Brother Joe called back into the room, "We have surprise visitors, Betsy!"

Betsy Barlow was a tall, big woman with huge

bosoms bulging over her calico apron. Around her stood three, four, five small children. Older ones crowded into the corners of the room. The Christmas tree was a branch of evergreen propped near the stove with popcorn laced through it.

Brother Barlow pounded Papa on the back. "Merry Christmas, good brother!" Annie thought she remembered seeing him and his family once at the church conference. "You don't mean to tell me that good wife of yours come up with oat cake and carrot puddin' again this year! Betsy, if the Lord hasn't blessed us to overflowin'!"

Betsy smiled a warm smile. "Won't you have some fried potatoes with us, Brother Wood?"

"No, I ought to be getting back by Annie's bedtime, and I don't know the whereabouts of the McLaughlins. I wonder if you could direct me?"

Because the room was so crowded, it was as warm as the Woods' hearth. It drew Annie into it until she almost wanted to turn her face up to feel the brightness and hear the Christmas music flooding her mind.

"Sure, sure! Yessir. Up two farms to Hill's Corners . . . you're . . . Say, wait a minute." Joe Barlow stopped short. "Better yet, ye'll have to come back by this way, and so I'll send Robert to show ye. Get your buckskin on, Robert, and ride with these good folk to the McLaughlin place. Sure, sure!"

Joe Barlow set his nose close to Mama's oatcake. "My, but that do smell heavenly. How's it goin' for ye this Christmas, John Wood? I hear ye're losin' yer eldest girl?"

"Yes, yes, I am. Hope you can come to our wedding party."

"Oh, do stay for a moment. Won't ye stay?" Betsy

implored. "Tell us about Clothilda. I heard little Liza Hamblin wasn't really in the family way. Just the girl's imagination. Clothilda must be happy!"

"Oh, we mustn't stay!"

"Yes, we'll be to that party, sure thing," he addressed his boy with the long face and ragged ears. "Now ye pay mind to the turning, Robert F., and bring John Wood and yourself safely back within the hour."

Robert, already in his coat, came shuffling in wearing his big leather boots at least three sizes too large. He kept his hands hidden in his pockets. "Come on, Annie." Papa ushered her through the door first.

"Good-bye," Betsy smiled. "Come and see us now, won't you, when you can stay? Tell Sister Wood thank you."

The cold air hit Annie going out to the wagon. She knew it was because she had been in a warm room still wrapped up. Mama said that always did it. She was chattery cold by the time she reached the wagon. She crawled into the collar of her big coat like a snail trying to draw into its house. Papa reached down and bundled her scarf around her ears more tightly while Robert quickly and easily climbed up into the wagon seat. But before he sat down, Robert reached out to help pull Annie up into the wagon. He pulled at her with both of his hands. Then Papa lifted her from the back while she fumbled for her footing on the wagon board.

When she drew her hands away from Robert, she still felt the imprint of his gnarly fingers through her mittens. He had no gloves. His fingers had been hard like knots in a hemp rope. When she sat down next to Robert she did not know why she felt so uncomfortable. It was not the same feeling as if her brother Peter had sat down beside her.

When Papa climbed in, he settled down with some difficulty. "Will there be room?" he asked, looking at them both. Annie sat as close to Papa and as far from Robert as she dared to sit. But neither of them answered.

"I guess there's room. Well, we're off then. Har!" The horse plodded ahead when Papa snapped the reins.

The air seemed very different. Robert's presence changed everything. Though his hands had let go of hers, she could still feel the pressure of those bony fingers. It was strange to her that she could still feel the grip of his hands. She curled into her coat, glad for Papa's black bulk next to her. Yet she could sense Robert as though he were a big rock weighing down the other end of the bench. When he said nothing, his very soundlessness made her feel nervous. Neither Papa nor she felt like humming, and yet the quiet seemed so heavy each of them would have welcomed a break in the silence.

"You going to school yet, Robert?" Papa finally asked.

"No."

Robert must have been at least two years older than she was. His hair was heavy and dark over his ears. On the back of his neck it curled and almost glistened in the moonlight. Annie watched his knees next to hers. They were relaxed and open. If she turned her head slightly, she could see his face looking toward the fields.

"Hadn't you ought to be going to Circleville to school?"

"I don't know."

"It seems to me you ought to go—at least some of the time, son."

Moving along in the lonely countryside under the bright moon, she tried to understand what it was that made the air so different. Robert reminded her of his house—dark with something that was probably lighter inside. She wanted to shake Robert and make him talk to her and look at her.

In a moment he finally did say something. "Turn right here, sir." There was a strange round tone to his words. "It's the third farm."

There was a brightness in the McLaughlin place while Papa delivered the basket. The little children squealed with delight, and the baby tugged at Annie's coat. Papa had the same hard time getting away as he had with Robert's family.

On the way back to the Barlows, Papa talked and talked because he knew Robert wouldn't. He talked about farming and cattle and making sure the hay wasn't too wet when it was bundled into the haystack or it would rot. Because Annie was not very interested in the conversation, she watched Robert. As they reached his house set back in the trees, he turned toward her and caught her watching him. Her heart beat hard, and she instantly lowered her eyelids. He must have known she had been watching him—his dark hair over his ears, the rough skin on his cheek.

When Robert leaped down into the snow, Papa called after him, "Remind your folks to come to the wedding party. You young ones also if you've a mind."

Robert looked up and nodded. Still, he didn't say a word.

"Thanks for your help, Robert."

As they pulled away from the dark house, Annie noticed that everything had returned to normal again.

12

The wedding made it a bigger Christmas than it had ever been. There was more of everything—more relatives coming and going, more baking, more talking and planning.

For several days Aunt Celia and Aunt Martha and some cousins helped Till and Mama bake pies, bread, candies, and cookies. Annie had never seen so much food. Till fixed the stuffing for two big turkeys, and Papa brought in a big ham, a leg of beef, and a lamb. It looked like they were going to feed Johnston's army, Papa said.

Best of all were the honey and molasses cupcakes baked in the muffin tins. One of the cupcakes had a thimble baked inside of it, and the other a ring. Till explained to Annie, "The one who gets the thimble will be an old maid or bachelor. The one who gets the ring will be the next to marry."

"What if I get the ring?" Annie asked Till.

"Then we won't be having another wedding for a long time, will we? Unless you were thinking of getting married right away?" Till winked at her while she smoothed frosting over one of the little cakes.

Annie was quite sure she would not be getting married for a long time. But she would like to be the one who got the cake with the ring in it, all the same.

On the day before Christmas several sets of relatives arrived from Kingston. Grandpa and Grandma Volney Johnson and a whole raft of cousins swarmed over the yard, stomping in the snow and singing at the tops of their voices, *Jingle Bells, Jingle Bells.*

Mama, Martha, and Celia were hard put to find enough bedding in their household and enough space on the floor to bed everybody down. The Wood children gave up their beds to the grownups and got ready to sleep on the scattered rugs. When bedtime came, Annie could not drift into sleep. Or if she did, a cousin would stir, and she would wake up. Then she heard voices below her and strained to listen.

From the kitchen Annie heard Mama say, "Till, honey! You're still up? I had no idea it was getting so late. Till, you must get some sleep."

Annie heard Mama's footsteps moving close to Till. Mama was clearing up some of the dishes or helping Till with the cakes.

"I don't feel like sleeping," Till said so softly Annie could barely hear her. "Mama, I'm so afraid."

"You're afraid of what, sweetheart?" Mama whispered.

"Oh, I don't know. Afraid I won't be Till anymore."

For a while Annie could not hear what Mama was saying. But Mama's voice moved closer to the stairway.

"You'll always be our Till, sweetheart. But you'll be part of a new family too." There was a long pause as though Mama and Till put their arms around each other. "We've got to get some sleep, honey. You have a big day tomorrow. Go to bed now."

In a moment Till was in the bedroom, picking her way among the bodies on the floor—Annie's included. The only one she couldn't get past was two-hundred-pound Corinda planted firmly in front of the closet where Till's nightgown was.

"Mmmmmmugh ugh ugh." Corinda snored.

"Get up!" Till joggled Corinda's shoulder. "Corinda, you're taking the space of three or four people."

"Ummmmmpgh."

"Ohhh . . ." Till grumbled in a Papa-like suppression of anger. "My last night at home and I can't even get into my nightgown." Tearing off her apron, she fumbled for her quilts on the floor and lay down in her dress.

Annie watched her sister's face in the milky moonlight from the window. Across the room full of sleeping cousins, they were the only ones awake. Till was staring at the ceiling. Annie wondered what she was thinking. This would be her last night in the Wood house. Tomorrow—Christmas day—would change everything. She would belong to a new family all of her own. She would no longer be Till. She would be "Till and Rye," part of something new.

When morning came, Annie woke to Mama's voice and the voices of the other aunts making things ready. There were more gifts than Annie had ever seen on Christmas before. Annie was surprised, along with everyone else, to see the pretty tree in the parlor by the hearth. After oatmeal, when Papa lit the candles and everybody knelt to say the special Christmas prayer, she could not shut her eyes. The world was too bright and lovely to miss any moment of it. Till looked happy.

After Uncle Dan prayed, Papa read the story of Jesus out of the Bible, and Aunt Celia led a few carols. Then Mama let the children try on their new Christmas wedding clothes. Annie had never been more excited. Her new dress was sprinkled with such a shower of pink flowers that she felt like a queen in a garden as she waited for Mama to tie the big sash.

"You look pretty," Mama commented.

There was such Christmas magic! Was it real? Annie turned and turned and bounced and laughed in her new dress.

Christmas morning was wonderful. But even more exciting than Christmas morning was Till's wedding in the afternoon.

At about two o'clock the family gathered noisily in the front room. It was so crowded that people were standing three and four deep. Hanging back behind Aunt Dora's chair with the cousins, Annie stood on her toes so she could see. Old Cousin Jenks played a little melody on the violin. Then Papa stood up and began to speak. "We welcome you, our close family, to our home for this special occasion. Let us pray." Annie bowed her head.

It was a long prayer. A prayer for happiness, a prayer that extolled the virtues of Till and Rye, that implored the Lord to protect them from evil influences, to guide them into paths of responsibility and righteousness.

"And our Father, please grant them the wisdom to travel to thy holy house in due time to be sealed up unto thee forever."

Annie had never seen a wedding. When Rye gave Till the wedding band, she half expected him to yank his bride into his arms. Instead, he gave Till a short peck on the mouth.

Then that was all there was to it? Annie wondered. She tried not to think about Burton's crude words, or about Rye's first kiss in the yard under the cut up apple tree. She felt relieved. She stood staring at her sister in the white dress. So then everything was going to be all right after all?

Till hugged Jennifer and Laura around the neck, and Jennifer began giggling. The three girls went into the kitchen to help Mama where Annie couldn't hear what they were saying.

In a few moments a few of Rye's friends drove down the drive with a mule and buggy, carrying wedding presents with them. Balancing the presents under one arm and pumping Rye's hand with the other, they laughed and made fun of Rye.

"You're a married man now."

"You did it. You finally did it."

"Yeah. I did it," Rye smiled good-naturedly.

Soon more of Rye's distant aunts and uncles and cousins drove in from Circleville. Mama had John take their coats into the boys' bedroom because there wasn't room for them downstairs. Soon the people from the church came. It was good the weather was not too cold, for there were so many guests wishing Till and Rye happiness they spilled outdoors.

Till was radiant as sunshine. Her eyes were moist as though any minute she would burst into tears, but Annie knew it was not because she was sad.

"Now you're all set up to begin on life's road to happiness," the aunts told her as they came to kiss her.

Just before supper Till and Rye sat down on the settee beside the hearth. Rye took Till's hand and inspected the ring on her finger. Softly, Rye whispered something in Till's ear. Cousin Frank Olson suddenly crept up behind the settee and dumped a big box of rice over Rye. Startled, Rye and Till jumped up and brushed the rice out of their hair and clothing. But they were laughing. Everyone teased both of them.

Old Jenks finally struck up a tune on his old fiddle, and Rye whisked Till onto the parlor floor to dance.

A few others joined them. It was crowded, so most of the guests just tapped their feet.

Finally Mama announced that supper was ready, and while everyone stood still where they were, Papa gave another long, solemn prayer. "And dear Heavenly Father, please bless Rye and Till that they might always have the gift of thy Spirit to guide them—that soon they will be able to be sealed."

Annie watched Till and Rye out of the corner of her eye. They were holding on to each other.

"Let us all be mindful of our own stewardships and our responsibilities to strengthen the bonds of love among us and to consecrate ourselves to thy eternal kingdom."

Annie was bored by the time the prayer was finished. And hungry. And so was hefty cousin Corinda, for Annie saw her eyeing the food during the prayer. When Papa was done, all of them descended on the big platters as though they were starved vultures. There was turkey, ham, lamb and beef, big hot noodle casseroles, fruit salads, boiled carrots, scalloped onions, baked potatoes, hot bread pudding, corn bread, and scones. There was more food than Annie had ever seen in the house at one time. And more people. Most of the families from the church came. Annie saw Mr. and Mrs. Barlow, though they hadn't brought Robert, or any of their children.

While everyone ate there was a ripple of light talk and laughter, but the people soon filled up with food and began clapping their hands and singing, *For he's a jolly good fellow, for he's a jolly good fellow.*

To be a good sport Rye danced the highland fling. Everyone clapped except Till, who looked embarrassed. Annie was standing close beside Papa and Uncle Dan, and Papa said, "Well, he thinks he's somebody. . . ."

"Growing pains! Aware of himself—but he hasn't quite fully harnessed his powers yet," Uncle Dan declared. "Marriage will make a man out of him!"

"Rye!" Till whispered, trying to get his attention. When Rye turned toward her, she drew him back into the crowd.

"Ha! You can sure tell they're a married pair!"

Soon somebody cried out, "The wedding cakes! Let's see who will get the ring in the wedding cakes!"

"The wedding cakes, to be sure!" Mama exclaimed. She and Dora went back into the kitchen and brought out dozens of the little dark frosted cakes on cookie trays. Everyone had one. The cake was delicious. Everyone hoped to find the ring inside of theirs. There was nothing in Annie's.

"Who has the ring . . . the ring!" Uncle Dan shouted.

Back in a corner Annie saw Corinda Wood with almost all of her cake stuffed into her mouth at once. "Argh . . ." she mumbled loudly. Soon she could speak. "I think I got it!" she cried out. And she was right. Out of her mouth she plucked the ring still covered with cake crumbs. "The ring . . . the ring!" Annie wondered if Corinda would really be the next to be married.

"Any prospects?" Uncle Dan shouted.

"She does have a boyfriend," Aunt Celia grinned.

"Corinda has a boyfriend. Corinda has a boyfriend," George, Emmett and Frank chanted.

"Who has the thimble?" Mama's father, Grandpa Volney Johnson wanted to know. There was another hushed silence among the people in the parlor.

"Well, I'll be blessed!"

"Who is it?"

"It's Rye! It's Rye Hadley who has the thimble."

"What's this supposed to mean?" Rye shouted, removing the thimble with a flourish.

"Boy! It means you'll never be married!"

"Aha! The joke's on Rye."

"It's a joke all right," Rye laughed. "Ha! A funny one! Still free as the breeze? Never really married to Till? What an arrangement!" He grabbed Corinda who was the closest girl cousin standing by and pretended to dance with her. "Just a lover forever," he grinned, spinning her around.

"He's not quite used to being a married man yet," Uncle Dan laughed.

Till's face was flushed. She laughed, a weariness in her eyes.

"Well, it's been a great day," Papa boomed.

"And it's time all of us got to bed," Mama added.

"Glory. It's getting late for the kids! We do need to get home," Grandpa Volney Johnson proclaimed.

Annie was so tired, she was glad the party was almost over. They had all had a good time. The aunts converged in the kitchen and began clearing away the dishes. A sudden quiet settled over everything.

Aunt Celia sent all of the children who were to stay all night to the upstairs bedrooms. Mama said the last good-byes and gathered up the last cups and plates. Annie was yawning as she climbed into her bed on the floor. The place on the bedroom floor where Till had slept the night before was empty. *Where was she now?* Annie wondered. *What will happen now?* Till wouldn't be coming home anymore.

Finally she heard Mama, her voice sounding teary. "Thanks for waiting, Till. Good-bye, sweetheart."

Even though it was cold out of bed, Annie stepped

gingerly over the people on the floor and shuffled to the window in the big slippers that used to be Till's. Looking out on the frosted world aglow and shadowy under the moonlight, Annie saw Till and Rye standing near the two-seat buggy. Rye took Till by the waist and lifted her up. Then he climbed up on the other side, took the reins, and snapped them over the horse. The animal pawed the ground, snorted, and trotted away.

Now the house was quiet, and she could hear Papa and Mama and the aunts and uncles getting settled downstairs. She snuggled down again into the covers.

But she couldn't stop thinking about Till and Rye, the party, and all of their friends. She thought about Mr. and Mrs. Barlow dressed in their best uncomfortable clothes. And in a curious moment she felt disappointed they hadn't brought Robert along.

13

A softness brushed Elizabeth Ann's cheek. She forced open her eyes. It was Robin with her doll. Behind her were Clara's boys, Lowry and Kurt.

"My baby loves you, Grandma," Robin said.

"How nice," Elizabeth Ann whispered. "Hello, boys."

"Hello, Grandma."

"I had some visitors."

"There are a lot of cars parked out front."

"I don't mean those kinds of visitors. . . ."

"What kind?" Lowry asked quickly. He sat by the bed and took her hand.

"People in white robes standing at my bed. You see? A young couple." There was a moment of silence. "And a mother with her baby. She showed me her baby. I didn't know who it was."

That young man. Was it Rye Hadley? They had waited and waited for so long to hear that Rye had taken Till to the temple, but it did not happen.

"You know . . ." She felt Lowry's hand on hers. But she couldn't say any more. She remembered how sad she had been when Rye and Clothilda had slowly left them after the wedding. And in the years after that, the Hadley family had left the Church as well. But now she thought she had seen Rye. He had come back to tell her *something. Yes, that must be Rye. But she did not recognize the woman. She could not imagine it was Till. Lowry pressed her hand. She closed her eyes.*

There had been a difference in the house after that Christmas, an emptiness filled with a certain kind of hope that Till would come again and slip into the big bed with Laura and Jennifer to giggle with them over little things Annie could not hear them say. There was a difference at the morning table where Till no longer came laughing and swinging her skirts, or singing and whistling tunes with Mama while they stirred the washing in the tub.

Laura and Jennifer huddled together and snickered over Till's letters, asking Papa to let them open each one and take the first turn. They had things to say to each other that Annie didn't understand. So she left them alone.

John and Peter were always gone with Papa, so Farrell and Annie stayed together with Mama by the warm fire while she carded and spun, or knit the yarn into warm shawls.

Annie took her knitting out of her patchwork bag and sat with it for hours. It hadn't been long enough to give to Till at her wedding, so for her wedding present she had made little mats out of dry grass to put under hot dishes on the table. Mama helped her make them, telling Annie that she could still turn her knitting into a lovely blanket for Till's first little child when it came into the world—beginning like a lump under Till's apron the way children came, although it was puzzling how they got there.

"It's what happens when people get married, Annie. Children come and then a new set of troubles.

Things change. Nothing stays the same." When Till and Rye married, he had taken her out of the family. Having a baby would make a new family. "We keep having new ways to grow," Mama explained.

Sometimes it was almost as though Till had never lived there, and then Mama would say, "Take this old apron of Till's with you to feed the chicks, Laura," and they remembered Till again and the house began to feel empty. After Papa brought a letter from Till, there was talk about Rye and Till and how they were getting along in Circleville now, how long they would stay before they went to Idaho, and how they must come soon for a visit. But they did not see Rye and Till, even when spring came.

The trees were well into blossoming before Rye and Till came to the house again in a big new wagon hitched up behind two big bay horses.

"Mama! Mama! Farrell! Annie!" Till cried. Annie had never seen Till so excited. She rushed so fast across the driveway that she slipped on the gravel. "Mama! Oh, Mama!" She seemed to have tears in her voice. "I've missed you so dreadfully!"

Suddenly things were the same again. Papa and John and Peter came out from the barn behind the house rubbing their hands clean and laughing, and Papa took Till up into his big arms and swung her off the ground until she squealed with delight and rubbed her cheek against Papa's whiskers.

None of them noticed Rye until he led the horses back to the barn. Having Till at home seemed to make the family complete. Things seemed all right again—almost.

In a couple of days Till would have to go back in the wagon with Rye. The family evenings—the singing around the fireplace with Till's voice clear and high behind them—all came to an end too soon.

On the morning of the day Till was to leave, Annie tried to follow her around so there would be some last good memories. But she was in the kitchen when she heard Papa walking back and forth, back and forth in the front room, having a serious conversation with Mama and Till. Annie was not sure what he was saying.

"It seems a little risky to me. She still needs lots of looking after."

"Well, but I don't think it would hurt anything." Mama's voice came across hesitantly.

"Oh, please, Mama," Till begged.

"Well, you ladies decide," Papa banged the cup against the bottom of the water bucket, trying to get enough water to take a drink. "You decide. I got to get your meat and cheese in the wagon. I'm not much for it, but if you're sure you can fill the child with a nourishing meal once or twice a day, and you have a place to put her in the evening, well, it'll be all right with me. I don't see how Rye can get the food on the table for two, let alone three of you. My word, he sure borrows enough from us. It's lucky we had a few pounds of cheese to give him!"

"Now, John. You know this is the first time they've asked for anything. This isn't the place to belittle your son-in-law and him not present."

Annie could see Rye outside the window packing things into the wagon and rubbing down the horses to get them ready for the long ride. His big shoulders moved smoothly beneath the buckskin coat, and his thick legs marched firmly around the wagon, picking up his big boots as though they weighed nothing.

Papa left, tossing the tin cup in the sink.

"Mama, does Papa mind giving us the meat and cheese?" Till asked.

"Heavens no! Not on your life. He's glad to be of help to you."

"I . . . we do need some help. Doesn't everybody?"

"Till . . ." Mama hesitated. "Are you happy, Till? Are you really getting along all right?"

For a moment Till was quiet. "I'm getting along all right, Mama. It's just . . . I guess I'm learning like everybody else. Rye isn't perfect." There was silence.

Annie's ears seemed to hurt because she was straining so hard to hear. She wanted to go into the front room, but Farrell was tugging at his shoes, and so she knelt to help him.

Then Till sighed. "I've been so homesick, Mama. That's all. Please let Annie come back with me."

"She's the logical one, all right."

"Then it is settled?"

"I guess so. Of course, you'll have to ask her, too."

"Oh, Mama, you're grand!"

Annie felt a sudden jerk at her heart, and her fingers slipped with Farrell's shoe strings. The room, crowded with sunlight, seemed to be turning in circles in front of her eyes. She swelled up with excitement.

"Annie! Annie!" Till called, and she burst through the doorway and up behind Annie with breathlessness in her voice. She knelt and took Annie's arms in her hands. "Annie, how would you like to come and see my little house and keep me company? Oh, Annie!" With sudden warmth, Till pulled Annie up close to her. Annie could smell a strange mixture of clove and cinnamon in the dark smooth hair.

"Oh, Annie. You can come with me! It'll be such

fun. Oh, I'm glad. Get your clothes together. I'll show you my little garden, and you can see the lambs and pigs and help me take the rocks out of the beans!"

Without knowing how it happened so quickly, Annie was in Mama's arms telling her good-bye and promising to be a good girl while she was at Till's house in Circleville. Till was packing things neatly into Annie's small patchwork bag and drawing up the string, her hands quick and happy with excitement.

"I'm so glad. Oh, Annie, we'll have such fun."

For a while Annie was numb with eagerness and wonder when Rye lifted her into the new wagon behind the big bays. She looked down into Mama's face where she stood holding Farrell in her arms.

"Be a good girl. Make your bed and help Till with the dishes."

"Bye, Annie." Farrell waved.

"Bye, Farrell."

The world seemed to be made of comings and goings, and so little time between one hello and the next good-bye.

"We'll take the best care of her," Till assured Mama.

"Oh, I know you will. I'm not worried a bit."

"Har!" Rye shouted at the bay horses. "Get up, there. Good-bye, Mr. and Mrs. Wood. Thanks for everything."

They were off, the wagon jerking crazily behind the big bays until they reached the smoother road where the wheels found ruts to rock in.

"We're off like a stampede!" Rye chuckled.

Till waved and kept turning her head until the wagon rounded the bend, and they could no longer see the house or the trees and the barn. When she looked down from the high seat, Annie caught sight of the rushing brown and green river of spring daisies streaking like sunshine into the other colors until she was almost dizzy. The lull of the motion and the freshness of the warm spring sun rocked and warmed her into a hazy silence.

"Annie, I want to show you the lovely quilt the Circleville ladies quilted for me. And we have two little baby lambs you can hold and cuddle up to in your arms! And Mr. Parkinson has a giant litter of fat little pigs all squealing and poking their snouts into their mother's belly. He said we could have one as soon as we come back."

"Have one for a *price*," Rye interrupted her.

"Oh, Rye. I thought he said we could *have* one. You mean he wants money for it?"

"He wants a good price for it. You've had free pigs from your pa for so long you think they grow on trees." There was an edge to Rye's voice. But Till shrugged.

"He knows we can't pay," she reasoned. "We'll be giving him potatoes. He said he'd take potatoes. And I'm the one who's going to break my back over those potatoes."

Annie felt Till stiffen. But her voice was steady as she continued. "Rye is going to plant a lot of potatoes in the early spring, Annie. And before we leave for Idaho, underneath the green leaves growing out all across our little field, there will be tiny new potatoes so good to taste you can eat them raw."

Annie smiled. It was the best part about spring, eating all the little things that came up out of the dark winter soil.

"Can I see the pigs?" she asked Till.

"Yes, indeed. We'll show you the pigs as soon as we get home. Or if we're home late, we might have to wait until tomorrow. What time will we be home, Rye?"

"Land, you're asking that already just as we get started?" Rye's voice sounded angry.

"I just wanted to know so I could decide whether we had time or not to bother Mr. Parkinson about the pigs when we come home."

"I don't rightly want to bother Parkinson about the pigs after the long drive. We'll be coming in late, and we'll be tired. Wait until morning." And that was all there was to that. Till didn't say another word about the pigs or anything else for a while. Neither did Annie.

It was getting late when they reached Hadley's dark fields. All around the little house that sat back from the road, Annie could see the soil lying in rows like the corduroy in Farrell's trousers. It was late, with the red sun sinking into the hump-backed hills, and the yellow dusk glazing everything gold, crowding the deep valleys with purple and blue.

Till's house was so little Annie thought it looked lonely. No trees stood around it. There was just house and field, with the sun drawing one long shadow across the road.

"We're here, Annie!" Till cried, jumping out of the wagon before Rye came to help her. "We're at our little home. I'm so glad you're here. Jump down, Annie!" Annie jumped into Till's arms. Till hugged her tight. "Let's go see the lambs."

Behind the house was one tiny shed and a rambling leaning wire fence. Behind the fence two lambs nestled in the winter grass and a thatch of old hay.

"They're just new and such a short time away from their mother." Till's voice was soft on the dusky air. The lambs were bony, their eyes bursting from their heads like four crocus bulbs not buried deep enough. The sound in their throats was a stifled far-away sad sound.

Till led the lambs into the fold, jerking the clumsy gate shut. She and Annie brushed the short scruffy wool with their fingers and rubbed the cold nuzzling noses with their palms.

After a while they both got up and went into the house. In the dim light from the two small windows Annie could see that there was only the one room. In the back corner was a big straw mattress on the floor. Beside it stood a stack of wood and the big stove with its massive oven and gaping wood box. The stove took up a big space in the room. Till's cupboards were just crates, whitewashed and draped with calico curtains. She had sewn little skirts of the same starched and ruffled calico for the windows.

In front Till had placed a table and two chairs. The big crate against the wall was probably filled with blankets and clothes and wedding presents.

The best thing about the room was Till's round rag rug, warming the floor with reds and yellows and greens. Annie could see pieces of all the clothes her family had ever worn. There was Laura's Sunday dress of cashmere and Mama's rosebud and green calico on a bright yellow weave, bits of John and Peter's Christmas shirts, and some of her pink flowering slippery cotton Sunday dress with the satin sash.

"We'll fix you a comfortable bed right up here on this crate, Annie, right beside the stove where it's warm. I have plenty of blankets and an extra pillow. Rye and I will be just over here, on the other side of the stove."

As soon as they came into the house, Rye put wood and paper into the stove and lit it with a match and kerosene from the lamp. It flared up suddenly with a gust of black smoke, and the air in the stove belched.

"Rye, you always do that with too much kerosene or something, and the smoke makes everything so dusty," Till objected, trying to cover her eyes. "Can't you just put a little oil in?"

Rye stopped prodding the fire and looked at her briefly. It wasn't a friendly look, but he didn't say anything.

Something in the air puzzled Annie. It wasn't the smoke. It wasn't the fading afternoon light. Soon the flames inside the doorway of the stove cast a gold sheen over the floor, yet there seemed to be a damp cold air filled with a heavy silence.

Till put on a pot of water and popped in three or four big potatoes cut up into little pieces. After a while she cut thick slices off the loaves of wheat bread Mama sent with them, then laid big slices of cheese on top of them, and set them in a pan in the oven to melt.

While the potatoes were cooking, she took all of her wedding presents out of the old crate to show to Annie. She had white linen napkins embroidered with silk thread and some genuine silver candlesticks. Then Rye showed her his checkers and let her run her fingers over the black and red squares on the genuine printed paper board. He told her he would teach her to play checkers "with the best of them" and by the time she left she'd have him beat all hollow. He laughed at that.

After a while the three of them sat down at the table. Rye dragged an old crate from somewhere out of a corner and offered a quick grace. Till took the potatoes off the stove and served the slices of toasted bread smothered with melted cheese.

Rye helped Annie mash and salt her potatoes, and they began to eat. But her first bite of potatoes stuck in her throat. There was something about the quiet in the room that kept the potatoes from going down very easily. The bread and the cheese stuck in the same way.

"Aren't you hungry, Annie?"

"You should have made some kind of gravy, Till. These potatoes were over-ripe," Rye complained.

Till was very quiet for a minute. Then she raised her eyes. "You want me to make some kind of gravy right this minute?"

"Suit yourself. You're the cook."

"But you're the one who wants gravy. Do you want me to make some gravy right this minute?"

Even though Till's voice was quiet, Rye's voice had a roughness in it as though he were clenching his teeth. "I told you, suit yourself, Clothilda. I just thought Annie isn't eating, and it could be the way you fixed the potatoes."

"We fix them like this at home all the time, don't we, Annie? She eats good at home. Of course, we have butter at home. But you made me promise not to ask Mama for the butter. You said we'd get the butter from Mr. Parkinson after you started planting the potatoes."

Rye shoved his crate back from the table and dropped his fork to his plate with a clang. "Well, are you asking me why she don't eat? Don't ask me why she don't eat! Good land! All I do is make some simple suggestion, and you have to go pointing out all the reasons why this and why that. Just leave it alone. Just forget it." After his outburst, there was complete silence. Till dropped her eyes to her plate.

"All right," Rye said in a softer voice, and then again, "All right," as if it were all right.

Annie's stomach felt tight as a knot. When Till

talked about Mama and the butter, she remembered Mama's face and little Farrell banging his fork. The tightness in her stomach spread up and up.

"Eat, Annie. There's a good girl. Papa says you must eat good."

But she couldn't swallow, nor could she speak.

"What's the matter, Annie?"

Tears sprang into her eyes.

"There, you went and made her cry," Rye accused Till.

"Annie, honey. You don't have to eat if you're not hungry. I'm sorry. There, there, don't cry."

But it was too late. Heavy tears flooded up inside of her and gushed out onto her cheeks until she couldn't stop.

"Oh, Annie, honey! What's the matter?" Till put her arms around her. Through all the tears Annie heard Rye's voice far away.

"You should let her do what she wanted. If she didn't want to eat, you shouldn't have made her eat."

"I thought she'd be hungry. Annie, honey, are you tired? What's the matter, honey? Something else is wrong. I've never seen her like this."

"You shouldn't have pushed her. You push too hard, Till. You gotta let up. Not everybody can eat all the stuff you fix."

Till's hand tightened while she held Annie close to her. "If you know so much, Rye Hadley, you do something about it." Her voice was hard now.

"Well, I didn't make her cry!"

"Rye, please." Till's voice had a sudden hurt in it. "Don't blame me for everything." She paused. Then she turned once more to her little sister. "Annie, honey, can you tell me what's the matter?"

In the confusion—their voices and her tears—Annie did not feel like answering Till's question.

"Annie, honey . . ."

"I want to go home. Take me home, Till."

"Good land," Rye snorted. "Look what you did now. She wants to go home."

"Rye, please!"

"Don't 'please' me. If you can't do a simple little thing like fix food the child can eat, you don't deserve to have her around. That was one thing your pa made plenty clear. Don't you remember?"

"Rye, please!" The break in Till's voice came now. "Please, can't you just leave me alone? I'm trying. Annie's just homesick. Haven't you ever been homesick? You push and blame me until I can't do anymore than go crazy. Everything I do is wrong. Can't you just leave me alone?" Till turned away, and Annie could hear the tears breaking in her voice.

Rye got up from the table, kicking the crate over. "Land sakes! I didn't mean to make you cry."

Rye went to Till and stood behind her just about ready to touch her, but he didn't touch her. Annie watched him, his hands restlessly fumbling at his pockets. For a moment she stopped crying.

"Till . . . it's . . . there, it's all right. I didn't mean . . ." And then his hands finally did come out of the pockets in his trousers, reaching for Till's shoulders and taking her arms. "Till . . ."

Till's shoulders shook with her silent weeping.

"Till, damn it!"

Till turned, her face down, her lashes wet with tears. She wiped her eyes with the back of her hand, whispering, "Don't profane in front of Annie, Rye."

"Oh, all right. I keep forgetting. I try, Till. I'm sorry. I won't, Till. Look at me. I'm sorry."

Rye turned Till all the way around until she faced him; her eyes were still lowered. "Till. Till. Look at me." Rye took her head in his hands, stroking her silky hair until her ribbon fell off.

"Are you all right, Till? I'm sorry. Don't cry. Whatever it is, whatever I did, I'm sorry. Hear? Don't cry." Unexpectedly, Rye was quiet, looking into Till's eyes. "Till . . . ," he whispered gently.

Till smiled a little. As soon as she stopped crying, Rye gave her a little pat on both arms, cleared his throat, and turned away. "Uh . . . Annie," he began, "time for bed. You'll get into those warm blankets on the top of that crate, and you'll think it's better than home."

"I put Annie's patchwork bag in front of the doorway."

"Till, you and Annie get ready for bed, and I'll take the scraps out." In a moment he was gone.

In the strange darkness all around there was a sudden vibrant warmth like the sun after a summer rainstorm. Annie's breath still caught with occasional sobs, but she was calmer and tired, so she let her arms and legs hang loose while Till's smooth fingers tugged at her shoes and the buttons on her dress.

"You're tired, little angel. You're plumb wore out." Till's voice was like a lullaby, falling from some place far above her. The music of her whisper grew lighter and more distant with every word.

"Sleep tight, Annie. You'll get used to it all. You're just homesick, little angel. I'm so glad you're here."

Annie felt the nightgown slip over her shoulders and brush like a shadow against her legs.

"Here are some good heavy blankets to put underneath, and we'll fold Mama's old quilt over you on the top. That ought to keep you good and warm. And put your pillow under your cheek. Lie a little bit further up, Annie. That's right It's been a big day. Good night little one."

"Is she asleep?" Annie could barely hear Rye's words as he came into the room.

"Before I got her into the bed," Till whispered.

The hard surface of the crate felt solid. Only the softness and motion of her own heartbeat told Annie that she was still awake. The shadows in the room tilted into tall and weaving shapes that looked like blowing corn stalks and wild flowers by the side of the road. The leaves brushed her, soft like Till's hands. Annie thought she could smell the lilacs beside the river at home. She saw her river now, moving and tangling with the leaves. The river moved into the distance, into an endless ocean.

Without knowing how it happened, Annie remembered a dream. In the darkness, her mother's face had appeared in a window, her white cheek turned against the glass while her eyes looked toward a ship far out to sea. "Mother, Mother," Annie had called. Though she spread her arms wide, she could not seem to reach her mother. Mama kept moving back and away, her cheek still white against the glass, and her eyes sad, searching the horizon for the fading ship. "Mother, Mother, where are you?" Annie's voice stuck, and she began to fall. When she caught herself, she knew she was in a different place and that a red fire was still snapping in the black stove. Suddenly she heard Till whispering, a bright distant whisper.

"It's little things. Ever so little things."

"You know I love you, Till."

"Shhh. Don't wake Annie."

"We won't. She's asleep."

In the darkness there was a softness now, folding over her and rising and falling like a soaring bird that had leaped over a cliff and was suddenly sailing out over the water without moving its wings. A vibrating silence swept over the room.

"Till."

"Oh, my love."

The velvet darkness hovered in the corners now, touched by occasional smoky light from the stove. Annie could not see the dark bed on the other side of the great stove. She turned toward the wall.

"She's stirring in her sleep."

"She'll be all right."

"I love you. I'm sorry if . . ."

"Shhh . . ."

For a few minutes there was nothing but the sound of quiet breathing. Annie's heart calmed into a long steady beat, and she folded herself into a deep slumber.

14

Elizabeth Ann looked up. Lowry was still holding her hand. Had so much time passed? Was it Rye, then? Was that the young man—Rye?

Till and Rye had never been sealed in the temple. Rye had finally taken Till away from all of them. All the way to California. No church. No family. But Elizabeth Ann had always believed Till would return. Till had asked for the elders before she died. No one knew what happened when the missionaries came into the hospital room, except that Till had asked them to give her a blessing. But that sole attempt had not put her in temple clothing—not prevented her from being buried in her navy blue party dress. Elizabeth Ann had leaned over the dark coffin and cried, "Till, my dear sister! My sister!" until someone had taken her away.

"I believe someone was standing there . . . he wanted to tell me something."

"It's all right, Grandma," Lowry said.

She clearly remembered that the family had done temple work for Till and Rye in 1944. But where had that young man gone? He had wanted to ask her something. . . .

Those next few days at Till's had been painfully quiet—except for Annie's crying. She tried to keep busy with sewing and visiting the animals, but even the animals made her cry. When she dared to go to Mr.

Parkinson's farm to pull one of the piglets away from the sprawling gray-bellied mama, it cried, wanting to be with its mother. When Annie put it back beside its wriggling brothers and sisters, tears crowded up into her throat again.

The littlest things made her cry. When the spring rain scattered the animals in the barnyard, Till took her quickly into Mrs. Parkinson's kitchen. Mrs. Parkinson was a big lady with round legs and no ankles.

"Would you like some bread and jam, honey?"

"She'd love some, wouldn't you, Annie? Tell Mrs. Parkinson thank you."

"Thank you." But the bread and jam stuck in her throat.

"What's the matter, Annie?" Till turned to Mrs. Parkinson. "She's just got the worst homesickness, and I don't know what to do for her. She doesn't eat."

"Poor little dolly. Would you like a glass of milk, little Annie?"

"No, thank you."

"Maybe you'd better take some milk, Annie."

But she just couldn't.

At supper Rye got out the checkers and spread them like soldiers in the black and red squares.

"Now, here's how you play this game, Annie."

"We're going to be eating in a few minutes, Rye."

"Hang the dinner. Annie and I are gonna have us a ripping game of checkers. Now, the object is to jump over my men. These are my men. Those are your men."

"Rye, we've got to set the table now. We can't let Annie go without dinner. She hasn't eaten enough to keep a bird alive. We'll play after dinner. All right, Annie?"

"Land, you pick the wrong times for everything,

Till. All right. I'll move," and Rye picked up the checkerboard ever so carefully with one hand underneath and the other steadying the edges so the little round soldiers would stay in their places. Then he carefully edged out of his chair. But all of a sudden his foot hit the leg of the table, and the checkers slid, crashed, and tumbled to the floor.

Rye swore. Then he banged the board together and kicked the checkers out over the rug.

"Oh, Rye, I'm sorry," Till said and knelt to help pick them up.

Rye fumed. "See what you made me go and do? We better find every last one of those checkers or somebody is going to be sorry. How we supposed to play checkers, Annie, if we keep getting swept off the board? Huh? You gonna help us pick them up or not? Don't just stand there. Let's find every last one, and the one who finds the most gets an extra helping of dessert."

Annie couldn't help it. The tears just sprang up and fell over her cheeks again.

"Whoa. No tears. No tears!" Rye's brow knit like her papa's.

She couldn't stop crying. Till stood and spread out her hands helplessly. "Well, I just can't do anything else. I've tried. I've tried everything."

"How about let's play button-button? Guess which hand has the checker, Annie, and if you get it, you won't have to pick 'em up. Fair enough?"

But nothing stopped the tears.

"She wants to go home, Rye. I've heard nothing but crying for three days, and I've tried everything."

Rye turned from Till to Annie. "Did you see Mrs. Parkinson's pigs today? Weren't they something?"

Annie couldn't answer him.

"She wants to go home, and she won't hear a word of anything else."

"I can't take her home," Rye objected. "I got to plant potatoes."

"I know. I know." Till sounded upset. "So what are we going to do?"

For a moment, the room was silent except for Annie's sobbing.

"Look, Annie. We can't have all this unhappy crying. We just can't."

Annie cried harder.

"We have to take her home, Rye."

Suddenly Rye smiled and picked her up. "Look, Annie. If you'll just be good until I get that potato patch planted, I'll take you home, and on the way home we'll stop in Circleville and get you a big bag of candy that you can share with Farrell."

There was a catch in Annie's sobbing while she listened.

"We'll get you a big sack of candy for you and Farrell. How does that sound? You've got to be good, though, until I finish planting those potatoes, or it's no deal. All right? What do you say?"

For a moment it was hard for Annie to say anything.

"All right?" Rye asked her once more, waiting patiently for her answer. Annie nodded. "All right. It's settled. No crying, or it's no deal. Remember—a big bag of candy."

When Annie thought about the candy, she grew quiet.

The next few days she followed Rye out to the potato patch. She watched Rye plant the sets in the dark rows of folded corduroy earth and tried to be patient. She watched the robins dart across the ground, jerking up the fat worms, round and slick and rosy-gray. But the time did not move fast enough.

Mrs. Parkinson's dog Tacky, who often ate the table scraps, would run for her if she threw him a stick or an old shoe. Sometimes he'd bring the stick back to her. Sometimes he just stood barking crazily.

Annie had tried to guess when Rye would finish planting the last row of potatoes. And her guess was close. When he was almost done, she ran breathlessly back to the house to tell Till she must get her things packed. Till explained it was past dinnertime now, and that she should wait until tomorrow morning because there wasn't time left today.

So Annie thought about tomorrow, trusting it was the day she would go home. She ate with Till and Rye and listened to their talking.

"Well, Annie is eating better now," Rye observed. "Are you ready for tomorrow, Annie? The patch is done, you know. Tomorrow is the big day." Rye pounded the table. "I feel good, Till, getting that patch in. Almost like celebrating!"

"You've done a good lot of work, Rye."

Dinner was much too slow for Annie. The evening was much too slow. Tomorrow was the day she had waited for. She would go home and hear Mama's voice, touch her warm cheeks, and spring onto Papa's back. Tomorrow she would be home with everyone—everyone except Till.

Annie spent a lot of time puzzling over the problem of Till. She knew home would never be the same as long as Till stayed here. And it looked like Till wouldn't even be taking the trip back to Coyote, because she was in charge of the Relief Society quilting party. It looked like she wouldn't be coming to the Wood house ever again. That was what getting married meant.

Till's long dark hair hung like taffeta across her shoulders. Her cheeks were smooth and rose-colored. She hummed softly while she worked.

Was it sadness that Annie felt? Sadness that she would be leaving this little house where she had slept on the crate every night and helped Till set out the silverware and pour the hotcakes on the griddle? She wondered. But her wondering didn't last long. All night she was unable to sleep much for the excitement of knowing she would be going home.

When she woke up in the morning, it didn't take her long to get dressed and ready to go. Till took extra time to bake muffins, and she enlisted Annie's help to pack some bread and cheese for the journey. "Annie, you're a precious girl. And you've been an angel since Rye promised you that bag of candy." Till winked at Rye.

"Don't wait up for me to get back," Rye said to Till.

"Can I expect you tonight, though?"

"Just don't expect me too soon."

The two big bays pawed the ground when Rye tugged on the reins.

"Good-bye, then."

Annie waved until the tiny lonesome house was far away against the morning green of the mountains.

Rye kept his word. In Circleville he stopped and got a big bag of candy while she waited, tapping her feet to keep them warm in the crisp morning air. The streets were filled with people going and coming. A group milling outside the store watched greedily while the postman jerked a huge sack of mail off a stagecoach and dragged it into the post office.

Rye came back with the candy and a little sack for himself. Not candy, though. Something to drink, he said. "For me. You get the candy, Annie. But we won't open our bags until after lunch. If you hold it, you've got to promise not to open it until I say."

On the road, Rye sang snatches of *Yankee Doodle*, and Annie clutched the bag of candy, staring at the road ahead. This morning's journey seemed longer than any she had ever taken. She wanted so much to be home, and she was suddenly lonely without Till or Papa, or anyone who was close. She didn't feel safe all by herself with Rye.

"*Yankee Doodle went to town, a-riding on a pony,*" Rye belted out happily. "We're celebrating, Annie. We planted the potatoes!"

When the sun was high, they ate their lunch of bread and cheese and muffins. Rye's singing made Annie long for home even more. While she chewed the bread, she clutched the bag of candy so hard the paper wilted.

"Rye . . . ," she finally hesitated.

"What is it, Miss Annie Wood?"

"It's after lunchtime now."

For a minute Rye didn't talk. Then he looked at her slyly. "Aha! I know what you been waiting for, Annie Wood." He took a second look in her lap. "Well, Annie, we've still got that candy. I know Farrell wants some. But you want to start on your share, right?"

Annie wasn't thinking much about Farrell. She nodded, her eyes still fastened on the road, her ears hearing only the *clip-clop, clip-clop* of the big horses taking her home at last. Though the road rippled and blurred beneath their feet, they still didn't go fast enough for her. "Let's have some candy, Annie. Let's celebrate. We deserve it for getting in the potatoes." Rye helped her open up the bag, and the strong, sweet odor of molasses and horehound wafted up into her face.

"Just a few pieces of candy. And I'll open my surprise, too." He reached down and pulled the dark bottle from under the seat board. He helped himself to the candy, then opened the bottle and sipped. "Ahhh . . ."

Annie popped one of the round molasses drops onto her tongue. It slipped and slid in her mouth. After a while she was thirsty. The candy was sweet. She wanted a drink, too.

"Oh, you don't want any of this," Rye said.

But the candy had made her mouth so dry.

"You sure you want some?" Rye asked. "All right, then." Annie began to take a sip. "Not too much," Rye cautioned. "It stings." He laughed when it hit her tongue. It was so overpowering she coughed.

She took another piece of candy, soon forgetting Farrell. And while Rye was not looking, she took another piece until the sweet, soft and tacky taste stuck against the roof of her mouth. Then she took another sip of the stinging drink. She was so filled up with the taste of sugar and fire that she felt as though she were slipping into a huge vat of molasses. She dreamed about it while the bees hummed and buzzed around her mouth and lit on her sticky fingers, cleaning their wings on Farrell's big wilted paper bag of candy.

She took another piece and another. Then another sip of the stinging water.

"Yessir, Annie. We'll have you home in another instant."

It seemed that Rye wasn't watching her. Or if he watched, he didn't care. So she took another piece and asked for another sip.

"*Yankee Doodle went to town,*" Rye sang. His faraway voice sounded like a scratch on the hot afternoon air.

"You still eating that candy?" Rye inquired. "Annie, you know something . . . I think you ought to have one time in your life that you can eat all of the candy you want. Since we're celebrating, let's make this the time." He took another piece and another sip. So she took another piece and another sip. And another. She was not sure how many. After a while, with the jogging, jogging, jogging of the wagon, she felt a sharp pain deep inside of her stomach and a drowsy sickness in her brain. She hurt at every motion of the back and forth, back and forth rocking of the wagon.

". . . *Riding on his pony . . .*"

A series of rising and charging pains beat and burst inside of her. Something wanted to come up, but it didn't come.

"*Stuck a feather in his cap . . .*"

Everything seemed so warm. The sunlight beat around her. Her eyes fluttered and then shut. Abruptly they opened, then closed, and then opened. Then everything seemed quiet.

"We're here! We're here, Annie Wood!"

She raised her heavy eyelids a little. Then more. Finally with great effort she forced them open enough to let in the dappling sunlight that blistered the grass around them. Home stood in front of her all splendidly solemn.

"You're home, Annie Wood! Wake up!"

Her head was reeling. Somewhere in the haze before her she sensed the presence of her papa in the front yard and she heard a pounding noise. A hammer pinged and crashed and thudded and pinged. And stopped.

"Good heavens! What has happened to Annie!"

Great hands took her down from the high wagon.

"Land of heaven! So this is how you return my

Annie, Rye Hadley. With a stink of whiskey! She's sicker than a dog! I should have expected as much from you." The words crowded together in Annie's ears. "You haven't shown me yet that you can handle any responsibility at all. I can't believe I ever trusted you with Till. Annie . . . Annie . . . What have you done?"

Out of her sweating hands Papa took the wilted shred of the paper bag—completely empty. In the back of her reeling mind, Annie was sorry, so very sorry.

For a moment there was quiet above and beyond Papa's choking anger. Then Rye spoke. "Mr. Wood, I surely am sorry. I don't know what come into us. We just couldn't help ourselves."

"You always were a man who couldn't help himself." Papa's voice was stone cold.

Voices around her twittered and clamored. "What happened? What happened to Annie?"

"Oh, this good-for-nothing, irresponsible son-in-law . . . I told you he couldn't take responsibility. . . ."

"Annie, darling." It was Mama. "Annie. Oh, darling Annie. What an outrage! John, bring Rye on into the house. Annie, darling!"

A scorching patch of sunlight crossed Annie's face; brilliant light stabbed at her eyes. Then she fell into a shadow and felt a shadow rising close above her. She was in the house, and she was rocking and swaying gently in warm arms.

"Annie, darling. How did you get so sick? Oh, heavens above."

Mama's arms were warm and soft. She could see the lace at Mama's throat and smell the sweet-sour bracing perfume of cinnamon and clove and buttermilk and dough.

Gentle fingers unlaced Annie's bonnet and shoes. She felt Mama's hands on her cheeks, a cool cloth washing her face. The bed came up beneath her, soft and curving like a thick cloud rolling and easing into the corners under and around her arms and legs.

Mama, Mama. Good to be home.

15

Perhaps Rye was embarrassed. That was the reason they never saw much of Rye after that. Again Annie saw the figure in the dimming light. Was that why she could not recognize him now? Or was she only wishing for Rye, after all? Then suddenly the light was swimming in a froth of hair.

"Grandma!" It was Robin. She bent over Elizabeth Ann's face with a soft kiss. A larger hand reached for her, and she held it with a strong grip.

"We'll see you, now. Rest well." A visitor was leaving. She didn't know who it was.

"Thank you."

Elizabeth Ann reached up. Those who were leaving kissed her cheeks and held her hands.

The light from the window illuminated another figure for a moment at the side of her bed. She was sure she was seeing Rye again. It must have been Rye. His eyes were soft blue and very bright.

"Did you forgive us, Annie? Till . . ."

Till. That was it. Till. Rye had taken Till away from them. The first move had been to Idaho. Mama had waited anxiously to see if Rye was really going to take Till to be sealed, for they had passed right by the endowment house in Salt Lake City on their way. She had written to them several times, saying, "The temple will soon be finished. You won't be far from it there. You could be among the first to go." They had never responded. One time they did ask Papa and Mama to come to Idaho. But Papa said no.

"No, I don't feel good about going." For a moment he didn't say why, but Annie knew it was Rye. He still didn't like to see Rye.

"Please, John."

"It doesn't matter much, does it? They're hardly part of us anymore."

"John!" Mama said.

"Well, if he keeps living the way he chooses, he can't take Till to be sealed—so we won't be seeing them even in eternity, will we?"

Mama's cheeks looked white as paste. "I don't think it's that way," she whispered. "I mean . . . we'll see Till, after all. . . ."

"Maybe," Papa looked off into the distance. "But I'd just as soon not go, all the same."

Mama's father, Grandpa Volney Johnson, who had moved in from Richfield, came to take Mama, Farrell, and Annie to see Till and Rye. They had written to Aunt Dora, who had also moved to Idaho, and asked if they could stay with her. Of course, Aunt Dora said she would be glad to see them. Annie could not kiss Papa enough times when she said good-bye.

"Go on, now. Go on with you!" Papa's eyes glinted with worry and weariness. "Don't let Rye do anything else foolish!"

"Mama! Mama! Annie forgot her knitting!" Laura stumbled down the stairs with Annie's patchwork bag and the knitting.

"Aren't you almost done with that knitting, Annie

Wood? It's been more than a year," Papa teased.

"Almost."

"You might make Provo by tonight if you get a move on," Papa told Grandpa Volney Johnson.

Mama seemed more anxious than usual to be off. "We'll get going soon as Jennifer wraps the grub box and the butter. Where's Jennifer?"

"Take care. Annie and Farrell, mind your P's and Q's." Papa called good-bye.

The traveling days were filled with empty fields, mountains in the distance, and silence. Sometimes they played games and chattered. Annie felt safe and happy with Mama and Grandpa Johnson and Farrell. If Papa had been along, it would have been perfect.

The horses made good time on the smooth roads. The first night they stopped in Provo, the second night in Salt Lake City. Annie had never been to Salt Lake City. She and Farrell were dazzled by everything. The world turned and rolled and thundered past them—newspaper vendors on the streets whooping and calling, high heels clicking on the boardwalks. Lights in the windows flickered and sputtered against the night air. Big buildings stood against the blue distance.

At last they saw the unfinished temple where Till and Rye were supposed to go—the temple Aunt Dora and Uncle Al had always talked about. But they had also said they might go to the endowment house first to be sealed to Katy and Pauline and the rest of their children. Stone by stone the temple was rising into a granite monument topped by spires. It took Annie's breath away. She had always wanted to come here. And now here she was with Mama beside her and

Farrell chattering wonderingly, his head bobbing and his arms waving.

Then north, farther and farther, through tiny mountain roads in Idaho, lumbering into Albion, the wagon ground to a stop in front of a big brick house. Aunt Dora rushed out into the road.

"Oh, you're here! Bless you, bless you!"

Mama and Aunt Dora fell into each other's arms. Jeremy lumbered behind her, and then Uncle Al.

"Do you like it here?" Mama asked Aunt Dora.

"Not so many memories," Uncle Al offered.

"I was sad to leave the farm in Coyote," Aunt Dora added.

"It still hurts all of us to remember. . . ." Mama began.

But Aunt Dora stopped her with a raised hand. She cocked her head and smiled. "But the children are ours now!"

"Yes, we've finally been sealed," Uncle Al said. "In the endowment house forever and forever."

"It just happened recently," Aunt Dora said. "And I wanted to surprise you when I found out you were coming."

They were sealed. It was so important.

Mama began to cry. "I'm so glad," she whispered. They embraced again. Dora seemed to be whispering a message in Mama's ear. When Dora released Mama, she looked at her with a furtive look.

When Mama spoke next, she sounded breathless. "I'm anxious, Papa, to get there before dark," she said.

"Then let's go."

"We'll see you soon, Dora."

Rye and Till lived in a tiny hired hands' house on the edge of town. It was like the tiny house in Circleville—too small for the family members to stay overnight. Mama told Annie they would be going back to Aunt Dora's to stay. Big trees shaded the house, shutting out the hot sky, their leaves stirring and shifting with the wind. Right now the leaves were yellow and brittle, edged with crimson. Breezes tossed them to the ground, spreading colored patterns over the grass.

Mama leaped from the wagon and ran toward the house stumbling. Annie was surprised at her hurry. Why? It seemed she had learned something about Till and Rye.

At the doorway, Annie could see someone—yes, Rye! His face looked grave. He shook his head.

Mama turned again to the wagon. "Are you too tired, Grandpa, to . . . oh, never mind. Please come in. You're tired. I'll get Rye to drive the children back to Dora's. Besides, I'd like you to be with me."

Grandpa Johnson lifted his feet over the sideboards and climbed wearily to the ground.

"Rye," Mama beckoned. "Take the children back to Dora's. And to think we were just there! I'll see you later, Annie, Farrell."

Something serious was happening. Annie felt sad she could not stay with Mama to see Till. Saying only a quick hello, Rye rocked the wagon as he climbed in. His brows were knit. His eyes seemed to sink back into his face. He did not seem to be the same Rye Annie remembered.

Annie said nothing and clutched Farrell's hand as they rocked with the wagon. No one said a word. There was something different about Rye than she remembered. There was no readiness in his voice or laughter in his eyes. His words seemed bent like straws in the wind, each curved and fallen with heaviness.

"Don't lean over the side of the wagon, Farrell."

His voice was strictly business. "We've got to hurry."

Why? Annie wanted to ask. But she hesitated.

Soon the horses stopped in front of Aunt Dora's big brick house.

"Get your things, Annie. Get your bag. Is that Farrell's?" Rye yanked on both of their patchwork bags until they came loose from the piles of packed things still buried in the wagon. "Get along now. Out. Out."

Annie could see Aunt Dora's face at the glass in the doorway. Then the big door opened. Rye boosted both of them down onto the drying grass buried in autumn leaves.

"Well, well. So soon?" Aunt Dora was surprised. "Sakes alive, Rye. Good luck, then."

Before Annie could turn around, Rye was in the wagon trying to stir the horses into a trot. Then he was gone, moving west toward the tiny house where Mama and Grandpa Johnson had stayed. And Till. There was something about the house and Till that had darkened Rye's cheeks and put worry in his eyes.

"Come in, children," Aunt Dora's voice was like honey, and her hands gentle and steady. "We have a big bed just waiting for two children to sleep in it. Al, show Annie and Farrell up to the front bedroom while I warm supper."

The stairs to the bedroom were steep like home, although they had been varnished to a glossy sheen. The front bedroom reminded Annie of the long-ago memory of Aunt Dora's house near Coyote where she had heard the angels singing when they took Katy away. Here there were no vines. Only one window looked out on the road, but it had a window seat. Blue violets in pots stood waiting for the morning sunlight.

Before Uncle Al had a chance to put their bags on the bed, Annie went to the window seat and, careful not to hurt the violets, lifted the curtain and looked outside. A jagged edge of mountains in the west crowded the sunset, as orange and rose as spring flowers.

"We have the prettiest sunsets here!" Uncle Al said kindly. "Now I think your auntie has some supper for all of us if you want to come down. She'll tuck you in when the time comes. I won't bother to take down the bed. My, Farrell, you're growing up into a big boy." There seemed to be a catch in Uncle Al's throat as he lifted him high into the air. "You'll be as big as Jeremy in no time at all."

Jeremy was all that was left of Aunt Dora and Uncle Al's big family. Jeremy alone had to make up for all the sons and daughters gone away. But Annie knew it would be just for this life, because now that they had been to the temple, they would have Katy and Pauline and the others forever.

When they came into the kitchen, Uncle Al was already sitting at the table waiting for Aunt Dora to put on the supper.

"We're just about ready, children. Wash up."

Uncle Al took Farrell to the wash bucket and rubbed his little hands with soapsuds. "You've made a long trip and likely have a few chunks of dirt under your fingernails."

A fire in the stove and light from two kerosene lamps threw a shimmering glaze over everything in the kitchen. The table was set with the big silverware. On the cupboard behind sat the same massive clock and dishes Annie remembered.

"Let's thank the Lord," Uncle Al murmured and bowed his head. It was like the dinner Annie remembered long ago, except that now they were without

Katy and Pauline and Mama. And Till.

"Dear Heavenly Father, we're grateful for the safe arrival of Helen and her father and the children. And we ask thee that thy particular blessing at this time might rest with Clothilda and Rye. Help us to be worthy of all the blessings we do receive. We're thankful for this food. Please bless it to our good that it might nourish and strengthen our bodies. In the name of Jesus Christ. Amen."

"Amen."

Dishes of creamed carrots and meat pies, apple sauce, and thick slices of homemade whole wheat bread passed by. But in all the talk about whether or not Farrell wanted butter and honey on his bread, or milk on his applesauce, or if Annie would have two spoonfuls of creamed carrots or honey or jam on her bread, there were some questions about Uncle Al's blessing on Rye and Till. Coming here seemed the end of a long journey, not only of distance, but of time. Annie remembered all the long days she had seen and the things the family had done together: the comings and goings, the good-byes and hellos of them all.

"Al, can you reach the milk? I think they would both like a little more milk." And then, "Are you all right, Annie?"

"Where's Mama?" Annie was worried.

"She's . . ." Aunt Dora stopped. "She's helping Till."

"Why can't we go to help Till?"

"You can. In a few days."

"Clothilda is not feeling well, and it's better for you children to be here with us until she feels a little better," Uncle Al said. "Let's get your carrots down, and we'll have chocolate pudding. Won't that be wonderful!"

"Where's Mama?" Farrell asked.

"Mama will be here soon. Maybe tomorrow. You can tell her what a big boy you were to finish all of your supper!"

Without Mama and with everything so quiet, Annie didn't sleep well. She wondered about Till's sickness. It must be serious. They had always been allowed to see her when she was sick before. Maybe she was as sick as Katy.

Annie lay awake and listened to Farrell breathing through his nose. When he turned over, the breath came through his mouth, quivering and sputtering. The shadows in the window seat bent and crowded the room. Beyond the open window the silent silver moon was circled by clouds, then visible, then hidden again. The curtains fluttered in the window breeze.

When morning came, Annie awoke, hearing soft voices that sounded like Mama and Rye.

"Well, let them sleep. They can visit in a few days."

"Did you say anything to Annie?"

"Not yet. We wanted to surprise her. Isn't it fun, Dora? I'm as thrilled as you are, Rye."

"Nobody could be as excited as I am." Rye's voice seemed unusually tender.

"Mama! Mama!" She couldn't wait until she reached the bottom of the stairs.

Farrell woke up and followed close behind. "Mum. Mum."

"Hello, angels." Mama's smooth cheek felt warm against Annie's lips.

"Well, if it's not my old checker partner up and about!" Rye's eyes were warm. "You like a game of checkers, Annie?" Rye's cheerfulness surprised Annie.

"You care for honey or jam on your cornbread, Mr. Hadley?"

"Both is fine. And lots of it! Yes, sir, we're old pals, aren't we, Annie? My, but you're growing bigger every time I see you." Rye had forgotten that he saw her yesterday. But yesterday he must not have noticed.

"Now I'll ask you all to sit down. Land, I hope we have enough pork sausage."

"It looks so good."

"Me and Till were both hungry as bears this morning and no grub at our house to speak of!" Rye laughed. "You hungry, too, Farrell?" He pulled Farrell's chair close to the table and tickled him. Farrell laughed. Rye was friendlier than Annie had ever seen him.

Annie asked, "Where's Till?"

For a minute everyone waited for someone else to answer. "At home. Asleep. Grandpa Johnson is with her," Mama finally said. Her eyes flickered with laughter. "Oh, I can hardly wait to take you with me, Annie. I want it to be a big surprise for you." Mama exchanged a brief look with Rye.

"Is Till all right?"

"Till is fine. She has a surprise."

There was a surprise with Till. A mysterious something that the grownups had kept a secret. It was probably not the kind of surprise she would have loved—like a rocking chair. Annie tried to be patient through all the whispering and waiting, through Aunt Dora's knitting and Uncle Al's pounding and Farrell's crying.

An eternity seemed to pass between that morning and the next when it was suddenly crisp autumn, and Mama came and bundled them both in their caps and coats. After Grandpa whisked them into the wagon, they drove into the west, to the same house in the trees they had visited a few days earlier. Now every leaf was bright, and the grass glossy with dew. In the yard the wagon jerked to a stop.

What was the surprise? The front door cracked open, and Annie saw Rye. Sunshine seemed to come from his face. His excitement flooded into the yard. It was certain she had never seen Rye like this before.

"Annie and Farrell! Come in! Come and see!" Rye folded his warm hands over Annie's. For a moment she felt just right with him. He led her to the house.

"Go in. Go in and see," Rye said.

The door yawned with the morning. Running ahead of Rye and Farrell, Annie skipped inside. Mama's eyes glistened. "Come and see the surprise!"

"Isn't he wonderful?" The sound of Till's voice came out of the darkness. Her eyes were misty with happiness. "Do you want to touch him, Annie?" A tiny bundle lay in her arms, small and rosy and feathered with dark hair. "Your first little nephew, Annie."

A baby.

Annie was speechless.

"Isn't he something?" Rye's voice was somehow softened, changed. "Our boy, our boy," he whispered.

For the next few days Annie began to see Rye differently. Was there something about him that Papa—and all of them at times—had almost missed completely? Annie thought there must be. Even Mama seemed to see a new Rye while she stayed in the house, holding that baby for hours and hours. One day she said, while Till and Rye were in the room, "A little spirit from heaven. Now you'll want to be sealed in the endowment house so all of us can be together always. . . ." It was so important to Mama for everyone to be together.

Rye cleared his throat. Till forced a bit of a smile.

"Oh, I don't know . . ." Rye said.

"John and I were hoping . . ." Mama began.

"Oh, Mr. Wood doesn't care for me much. He doesn't want to see me here, let alone forever."

Mama gave the baby to Till and changed the subject. "Farrell, don't stand on Till's rocker with your shoes."

That was the last time Annie remembered seeing Rye. When Grandpa Volney drove the wagon back to Utah, Rye took Till and the baby to California, and Annie never saw Rye again.

Until now—if that was him, the figure in white. But she still didn't believe she was sure.

Through the years Till and Rye had six babies. Once or twice Till had brought the children to a family reunion. But Rye had never come. Then after a few years, Till did not come to the family reunions anymore. Mama was heartbroken because they had not gone to the temple. She always said she wanted to keep Till and Rye's family forever as much as she wanted to keep everyone else. It wasn't comfortable going through life not knowing if everyone in your family wasn't with you always.

"Well, Rye had plenty of chances," Papa would say. "Plenty of chances."

"But maybe not the best chance," Mama would answer.

What did she mean by the best chance? Papa wanted to know.

"Maybe some people just need more than the usual chance. They need to see more than what we see here. Maybe in heaven . . ." She never gave up hoping.

Perhaps it was because Mama cared so much that Annie had always cared, too. She could never seem to stop caring. It sometimes bothered her a great deal. She had loved Till. She had wanted Till to stay with them as much as Mama had wanted to keep her. It seemed that Rye had carved Till right out of the family and left an empty spot. Annie would like to have been able to do something about it, but she didn't know what to do other than to pray.

For a while, as they received letters from Till, it seemed to bother Till, too. But eventually she got busy raising her children and busy with Rye, and no one heard very much from them anymore. Finally one year many years later in one of her few letters to Mama, Till wrote that they had been attending a new church—a Christian church.

Elizabeth Ann was married to Owen by that time, and had children of her own. She remembered the expression on her mother's face when she read the letter. "A Christian church, is it?" She had frowned. "I'd have thought Till knew ours was a Christian church."

"That isn't it, Mama," Elizabeth Ann had whispered. "That isn't it. Rye never really felt at home. . . ."

One day in March many years after her own children had grown, Elizabeth Ann had received the letter from Till's daughter Myrtle saying that Till had left the Mormon Church. She simply had not felt herself a Mormon anymore. She had found a new life in this new Christian church, and Rye had said he didn't believe Mormons were always exactly right. He and Till had never made it to the temple, anyway. Elizabeth Ann had read the letter and cried. Years later she had heard from the cousins in California that first Rye, and then four years later, Till, had passed away.

Though Till had asked for the Mormon elders to bless her when she was dying, she was still very much out of the Church and would be buried by a minister. The telegram gave the time and place. The news of her death had hurt Elizabeth Ann. She had sat on the couch and dropped the telegram to her lap. She could not imagine her sister in the coffin and probably in a dark coffin as she had seen others buried. And so far away. It felt dreadfully wrong to her.

She decided to go to California for the funeral. Owen sat still at the evening table with the napkin half-folded in his hand. "You're not going all that way just to see a funeral, are you? It's not like Till will know you're there. . . ."

Elizabeth had bowed her head and looked at the table. She felt alone. "She's my sister," she said, remembering everything. "I haven't seen her for years."

"So she wasn't a member anymore?"

"A member?" she whispered. "She's still a member of the family."

"All right," Owen had said. He had always been kind. She remembered that, too—Owen's kind face.

In California, at the funeral parlor, she had leaned over Till, remote and pale in the navy blue dress, and she had cried out, "Till, my dear sister! My sister!" The tears would not stop. The pastor had finally drawn her away.

Elizabeth Ann tried to focus on the light that flooded the room.

It had been in 1944 that the family had done Till and Rye's temple work. They wondered if the work would be accepted. But they would do it all the same. In the temple she had concentrated so hard on remembering Rye, especially that last moment when she had seen him holding the baby. He had been smiling, his eyes a bright blue. Something wondrous had been shining in his eyes.

Now Elizabeth Ann rose up out of her bed slightly. As the moments passed she became more certain that the man who had been standing in her room was . . . Rye.

"Please, Rye . . ." she began to whisper. She leaned into the light. Yes, that same face came into focus again.

"Is that you, Rye?" she confronted him, suddenly seeing him very clearly. "You came to talk to me and didn't even leave me your name. Where's Till?" Yes, now she was sure it was Rye. "I know it's you now, Rye. Please repeat what it was you were saying to me. . . ."

Rye's voice was the voice she had not recognized earlier, but in this moment it was clear as a bell. It was Rye's voice. "I said I wanted you to know it took us a long time," he said quietly. "But finally we have come together with your mama and papa. I wanted to ask you if you forgave us. We weren't much of an example. And Till . . ."

"Yes. Where's Till?"

At that moment Clara came into the room. Suddenly the white visitors backed away. Elizabeth Ann's feet felt uncomfortable. "Move my feet, please, Clara. There, that's better," she murmured.

Clara didn't notice Rye or the others. Just as well, Elizabeth Ann said to herself. Her daughter had never known most of these people. It seemed difficult at the moment for her to identify just who they were.

But now she certainly knew Rye. He stood waiting while Clara settled Elizabeth Ann's legs.

"I just come to tell you we found our temple work done," Rye said. "And thank you. I just hoped you would forgive us, that's all."

Elizabeth Ann was about to speak, when her eyes began to focus on a young woman who had been standing beside Rye. It was . . . yes, it was Till. She recognized her now. Till smiled and reached out with her arms. She was dressed in flowing white.

"My goodness . . ." Elizabeth Ann breathed in sharply. Her heart seemed to beat out of rhythm. She could not seem to talk very clearly. "Is that . . . oh, my goodness! Forgive you! Of course I forgive you. There was nothing to forgive. I always loved you, Rye." She turned to Till. "Till!, I know you now. Oh, my dear sister, I am so glad to see you once again!"

Till held out her hand. Elizabeth Ann sat up. It was time. And she was ready now. Tears crowded up into her eyes. In the Christmas lights she saw Mama and Papa, Uncle Al and Aunt Dora, Katy and Pauline. And there was Owen! Why, he had been there all the time. He had been one of those standing by, waiting with the others. She knew them now.

Papa stepped forward, placing an arm around Till and smiling at Rye before reaching out to take Annie's hand. "This has been a wonderful Christmas gift for all of us, Annie. We're together again."

Author's Note

It seems fortuitous that the married name of the great grandmother of my nieces and nephews was Read. Her name is almost a request to her descendants to *read* about her wonderful life of loving and forgiving, and her death, which was a miracle.

Born into the King family (and related to the famous musical Kings), Grandmother Read told her family much of what is in this story. Although this is a novel with fictional names and scenes, this grandmother as a child really did worry about her oldest sister who was lost to the family after marriage—and she really did hear the angel music when her cousins died. The request for the birds' eggs is true. There are many other true events in the story. But the truth that is closest to me is my own experience, of hearing my brother-in-law, BYU professor Lawrence Read Flake, tell how he was actually in the room when his grandmother talked about the visitors who came to usher her home.

I not only owe my gratitude to my sister Elaine and her husband for this remarkable story about the Flake ancestors, but sincere thanks to those people who have helped with the publication: to Curtis Taylor and Lyle Mortimer for help with the earlier manuscript, *Good-bye, Hello,* and to my early readers and friends, Jerry Johnston, Bruce Jorgensen, Don Marshall, Carol Lynn Pearson, Douglas Thayer.

For this special Christmas edition, I am deeply indebted to Valerie Holladay, my exceptional editor who makes such an outstanding difference in my work, to my daughter Simeen for her beautiful cover illustrations, and to the proofreaders and entire staff at Cedar Fort, especially Chad Daybell for his whole-hearted efforts to raise the quality of publication, and to miracle worker Georgia Carpenter for her invaluable suggestions and support.

Marilyn McMeen Brown, 2002

What Readers are Saying About the Work of Author Marilyn Brown

The Light in the Room

"... blends a style vivid and delightful with a theme insightful and moving."
Carol Lynn Pearson, author

"... attempts to bridge the rift between popular and literary fiction and does an excellent job of it."
Jerry Johnston, Deseret News

"... transports us back to a Mormon past that is vivid, tangible and hauntingly convincing."
Donald R. Marshall, author

"... creates many scenes and characters full of life, tenderness, and love."
Douglas Thayer, author

"The rocking chair, traditionally the symbol of old age, is given to Annie as a child, then passed on. ... Losses become endurable with ... the understanding of eternity."
Central Utah Journal Review

House on the Sound

". . . a talented wordsmith, the dialogue rings true, the descriptions shimmer with life, the characters are fully realized.
Andrew Hall, AML List

"I hope you decide to read this book . . . it is written with a subtle elegance that is deceiving . . ."
Jeffrey Needle, Irreantum Magazine

"I heartily agree with Bruce W. Jorgensen, who calls the book, 'a good read—funny, scary, lyrical.'"
Richard Cracroft, BYU Magazine

Ghosts of the Oquirrhs

"The story is a very good one indeed . . . richly imagined, exciting . . . a memorable novel which . . . establishes Marilyn Brown securely among the top Rocky Mountain writers of fiction."
Richard Cracroft, BYU Magazine

". . . beautiful gift of language . . . one of the finest examples of historical fiction from Utah that has been written in recent years."
Sally Taylor, poet

"No one spins a better tale than Marilyn Brown. . . . in language that simultaneously engages and delights."
Marilyn Arnold, author

The Wine-Dark Sea of Grass

"*Well-crafted novel . . . may be among those few works of Mormon fiction we call 'classic'.*"
Richard Cracroft, BYU Magazine

"*A very sensitive subject handled well . . . I'm impressed.*"
Douglas Thayer, author

"*. . . Best novel about the Mountain Meadows Massacre.*"
Lavina Anderson, author

All of these titles may be purchased from www.cedarfort.com. Or call 801-489-4084.

The author welcomes comments.
Email: wwbrown@burgoyne.com

About the Author

For her work, Marilyn Brown has won several Utah State Fine Arts awards, the AML First Place Novel award, and recent Publishers' House Critics' Choice awards. She and her husband Bill (six children, fourteen grandchildren), are founders and operators of the Villa Playhouse and Little Brown Theatre in their hometown of Springville, Utah.